POACHER'S P

SAMUEL MILLS

abuddhapress@yahoo.com

ISBN: 9798374994063

The following is a work of fiction. Any similarities to actual people, places, or events, unless deliberately expressed otherwise by the author are purely coincidental.

1

Odilio Brimble scrolled through Twitter in the gloom of his study, lit up by the glow of his laptop screen. He was browsing the comments — responses to his latest review of the 27th-storey London steakhouse, GALAXIAS — familiar angst working its way through him as he read each reply.

@Rubbles93: 'Only Odilio could attack such a tawdry display of oligarch wealth and still punch down on his target.'

@themullet11: 'Big getting divorced energy from Brimble these days.'

@Clax0nTheSmiths: 'He's always had that bottle-of-wine-ranting-at-the-TV vibe. Boring old snob, The Gent should sack him.'

Odilio sipped his gin and tonic and scanned the room. With its bleached white interiors, his study, at first glance, was like every other room in the large Regency house. His wife had spearheaded the renovation, described as 'modern rustic', but the furniture here was Odilio's: antique pieces kitted out with the curios of his travels, gifts, and family heirlooms. Mounted taxidermy trophies suspended on the blank walls gave the feeling of having wandered into a museum. Outside, the last of the evening light was fading. Odilio switched on the emeralite lamp next to his computer. The calming effect of his bath — the salts and scented candles — had been undone in minutes, but the alcohol was helping mitigate some of the tension. He continued reading.

It hadn't always been like this. Odilio had made his name as a skewerer of the politically correct. In 1992, whilst a trainee reporter at the Times, he'd phoned a hotly-anticipated vegetarian restaurant on the eve of its launch, warning them a bomb had been planted in the building, which would go off if they didn't put steak on the menu. This was pre-9/11: when Odilio was revealed as the 'prankster' he was made to pay damages for two days' lost trade. His editor had footed the bill, happy to cover the costs in exchange for the publicity the stunt attracted. Odilio Brimble was an overnight success. He went on to work for a string of publications, culminating in the position of Head Restaurant Critic for the London lifestyle and culture magazine, The Gent. He presented a TV show, wrote a series of books, and appeared on numerous radio programmes, cultivating the persona of a feisty restaurant critic, dishing it out with impunity for offence his audience could only dream of fostering themselves.

And then, nothing happened for years. The 2010s were a plateau, and a plateau — when it comes to a career — feels like a decline. Odilio still wrote the weekly column. He still made the occasional TV appearance. His agent called now and then to propose a book project, which meant regurgitating old columns, mashing them together in a hastily composed volume; slapping his face on the cover to squeeze some money out of the Christmas-stocking-filler market. His last book, 'Don't Get Me Started On Tofu!', hadn't even made the top fifty. It was embarrassing. He did not want to write any more embarrassing books.

His assistant had urged him to get on Twitter. She'd agreed to run the account for him; he had no wish to trawl through the opinions of nobodies. That was his position in the beginning, at least. Odilio couldn't remember exactly when he'd signed in to check what was being written about him. He knew his status as a provocateur — it was a personality of his making, after all. The real Odilio was far more mild-mannered. The Odilio of The Gent was almost a fictional entity; he understood the principal business of his craft was to entertain. And so for his entire career until then, Odilio fancied his image in the public eye as something akin to Marmite: that half the people loved him, ate up his every word, ripped off his quips to their friends as they tried to adopt something desirable they saw in him. The other half, he'd come to accept, loathed his plucky toffishness. In the end, like Marmite, no one cared either way. It was a deal he'd been comfortable with for years.

Odilio stroked his fingers across the touchpad. His unblinking eyes glistened with the light of the Twitter feed. The reality was no way near half and half, he was reminded. Nearly every comment was unrelentingly and viciously scathing of him. This was nothing like the disdain you might reserve for a sandwich spread — it was genuine hatred. The few he could call 'fans' were far more modest in their endorsements than his detractors were oppositional. A single positive comment stood out.

@Gimmins616: 'I like him lol. Tells it as it is. Pity the loony left can't handel it!!'

Odilio clicked Gimmins' profile picture. His bio read: 'Tank enthusiast. Hate Europe'. There seemed to be a factory producing these people, Odilio thought. With their penchant for the Union Flag: their aggressive, badly-spelt messaging seemed more about shitting on others than promoting anything positive themselves.

7

Odilio suspected his appeal an extension of this tendency: did the Gimmins' of the world really care about fine dining, about what Odilio Brimble had to say on the latest food trends, or did they just like that he rubbed the right people up the wrong way? Did anyone actually *love* what he did?

Odilio opened his email and scanned the inbox. He'd put off reading Cooper's email for nearly an hour. It was his policy not to check work emails after seven, but curiosity threatened to win over. Agitated by his browsings or emboldened by gin: Odilio could feel his discipline slipping these days. Social media had a habit of creeping under his skin. Like a virus he had no immunity to, it ravaged his mind without a flicker of resistance. In the past, he wouldn't have done anything that made him feel so bad for so long, entirely of his own volition, as scrolling through a crowd of digital hecklers in search of some elusive redemption. He'd meant to leave his editor's email unread until the morning, but here he was, unable to stave off the inevitable. Odilio's heart sank as he read the short line of text.

Come to the office next Thursday. Anytime after lunch. Quick chat.

Had his editor smelt blood? It made sense that management checked the social media accounts of their staff; it'd never been so easy to gauge a writer's popularity than to scroll through the comments on their latest piece. And if they did? Odilio was finished. The game was up. Whatever appeal he'd held in the paper-based years of the 90s and early 2000s was over. He was a relic of a bygone era — a hulking great dinosaur in a museum or perhaps just a manky old dodo.

Odilio reached for his drink. He leant back in his chair. Away from the light of his desk, the room was cast in darkness. A kaleidoscope of residual screening ebbed and flowed like a hallucination on the surface of his eyes. He let out a sigh. This was how he was spending his evenings: like a picnic under the sword of Damocles, waiting to give reason to his emerging, inarticulable self-disgust.

2

In the living room, Helena Courtenay was overseeing the arrival of her sculpture, which was so heavy it had to be lifted into the house by a crane through the first-storey window. Outside, on a quiet street of West London, a young man from the hire company controlled the operation from the machine's booth, as his older colleague gave orders from the living room via walkie-talkie. Helena was practising an improvised version of semaphore through the window. She knew from experience you had to be present for such undertakings: you never left men to 'get on with it' unless you wanted the job done to the lowest standard possible. You got your hands dirty; you did your best to encourage them. You made them work for every penny, and that was the job you paid them for.

The sculpture swayed at the end of the line. The craneman estimated it weighed three tonnes. The difficult part of the task would be removing the straps from underneath as it was lowered to the floor — even an inch drop could crack the expensive marble tiling. Foam cushions would help detach the crane bands. Helena watched on, scrutinising every last detail of the procedure. The living room was her chief source of pride in the house, of which she was entirely and personally proud. A misnomer, of course: its real purpose was a showroom for material riches — a room out of bounds to people, save for the occasional, exceptional guest.

The crane jolted forward following an overly keen lever movement. The sculpture jerked in reply. "Give it a minute," the craneman radioed his colleague.

Helena paced the room, studying the layout from various positions. Making right angles with her thumbs and index fingers, she held these 'L' shapes at arm's length, closing an eye to gauge a sequence of perspectives. Her baby-pink trainers squeaked on the tiles as she zig-zagged across the room. "Let me explain," she said, her face softening as she turned to the craneman. "This is the 'rule of triangles' principle. I watch a fantastic series on my iPad. The way objects are arranged in a room is one of the most important features of their design."

"It's a lovely room," said the craneman.

"Isn't it just?" She looked around at her carefully curated assemblage of artworks: the eclectic mix of sculptures, minimalist paintings; the series of deconstructed vases on mighty white plinths.

The Courtenay name can be traced to the book of Domesday. The family still owns much of the land they did a thousand years ago, including the estate in Henley that sprawls the Chiltern ridge. The Courtenays are as old as money can be, Helena will put it bluntly as if admitting to some familial disease. The detail buffers an image one might form of her as an aspirational businesswoman. But Helena is proud of her journey: proud to have decoupled from the trajectory of idling aristocracy. In a way, she retains the best of both worlds: the prestige of the Courtenay name whilst boasting a career that's seen her rise to become one of London's most important art dealers.

The sculpture stopped moving. Helena gave instructions as to where she wanted it placed. The craneman measured the base and marked an outline on the floor with tape. Helena scanned the room, left, re-entered — saw something she didn't like — then beelined for the tape, insisting it be moved slightly. Without fuss, the craneman struggled to his knees to relay the tape exactly where she wanted.

During the 1980s, Helena's father, William Courtenay, undertook a project to expand the family portfolio by investing in the emerging markets of Nigeria, Hong Kong, and South Africa. In the summer holidays at boarding school, Helena and her brother, Phillip, travelled the world, witnessing their father's knack for international business. "I received my education from that man," Helena would say. "He taught me that business is entirely about magnetism; there's nothing more to it than that." Indeed, it's a philosophy ingrained in her: to raise an aristocrat successfully is to produce someone with an instinctual sense of freedom. A consciousness shaped by minimal closure, it's a show-don't-tell business. To truly live free is to never have not been: to be unable to consider it any other way. This is how you step up to the provisions of the lifestyle without going mad. The next step is convincing others of its inevitability. Helena's real gift lies in making it seem there's nothing wrong with a world like this.

The sight of a crane protruding through the window — the portly man in the scruffy high-vis-vest — and the large sculpture dangling at the end rejigged Odilio's memory as he entered the living room. Helena must have mentioned its arrival a dozen times in the past week. He watched the man in the vest wrestle foam blocks from underneath as the sculpture descended to the floor. Helena signalled to the pavement; she gave a command to the man on his knees. To watch his wife issue instructions was to witness her in her element, Odilio thought. Helena had ordered adults around since the day she could talk. Her charm was a lifetime in the making. Odilio had been on the receiving end of this charm once, not as a member of staff but as the gentleman guest seated next to her at the 2004 Henley Royal Regatta. He remembered little else about that dinner other than he would have gouged the waiter's eyes out with a spoon if Helena had asked him to.

The foam cushions were removed and the sculpture settled. The masking tape was peeled from the floor. Helena turned to find her husband in the doorway. "Darling," she said, walking over.

"Sweetheart," Odilio replied sarcastically. She tugged on the lapels of his dressing gown.

"You've had a bath," she said.

"I was feeling brittle."

"You've had gin," she smiled. Odilio kissed her on the cheek. She was the last person he'd relay his woes to. An unflinching toffishness was part of his appeal. His editor's emails, the Twitter trolls — if she knew how much those things got to him, it would only cement, in her eyes, a weakness of character. The Courtenays were hardly ones to care what the little people thought.

The craneman coiled the line in a bundle, scanning the floor for tape marks. "We're finished," he announced.

"How excellent," said Helena. "You've been such a star."

"I'll be getting on, then."

Helena showed him to the front door, returning to find her husband digesting the latest addition to their house. "It's called Come and Get It — isn't it fantastic?" she said. Odilio's first reaction, staring at the massive artwork that now

13

took pride of place in the living room, was how ugly it was. A tacky, ridiculous thing — that, or he just didn't get it. When it came to modern art, Odilio was the first to admit he didn't understand it at all.

"It looks like a big turd," he said.

"I thought you might say that," Helena frowned. It was unusual, she could concede. A large swirl of porcelain conjured up an image of an ice cream (or worse) sequinned with thousands of heart-shaped crystals, topped off with a bronze statue of a naked woman with exaggeratedly large breasts. "I think it's brilliant," said Helena, walking up to the sculpture with an expression of awe. "Elias isn't afraid to go big because there's such a softness to his work. His sculptures have this kind of regal sensitivity, like the temperament of elephants. Do you know what I mean?"

"Not really," Odilio yawned. He was feeling sad and peckish.

Helena studied her husband. "Come here," she reached out her arms.

Odilio hesitated and doubled back.

"Is everything okay?"

"Everything's fine."

"You've been in your study a lot lately."

"Working," he glanced at the floor.

She ran her hand along the side of his face. "Are you sure?"

"I've been busy." He filled in the absence of his wife's reply: "Getting my head around Twitter."

"Well, I hope you're not getting obsessed, darling. There's nothing more boring than the internet, don't you agree?"

14

"Agreed," he swallowed. Helena leant forward to kiss him. "And where's Tabitha?" he asked. Usually, at this hour, their daughter could be found charging around the house in the throes of some energetic game with her au pair — a last crescendo of activity before bedtime, notable, suddenly, in its absence for the strange silence imparted on the house.

"Rachel's just putting her to bed. She had her first session with the tutor today. Apparently it went really well. I think that and the shock of going back to school yesterday has rendered her exhausted. She's having an early one tonight."

"I could do with an early one, too," grunted Odilio, who tightened his dressing gown before making his way downstairs to the kitchen for some cheese.

3

Odilio rang the buzzer; the door latch clicked, and he entered. Rarely did he visit The Gent's offices in Bloomsbury. For the best part of his time at the magazine, he'd worked from home. Other than the annual work drinks, it was only the occasional meeting that brought him into town. The office was filled with the underlings of the magazine's actual writers. Odilio took a seat in the waiting area. His assistant — a young woman called Amy, who'd come to exist in his mind as an email address rather than a human being — popped by to tell him his agent had been in touch and that they were pitching a book idea for his consideration. 'The Ten Bird Roast' would be a journey of personal and cultural discovery. A culinary voyage involving the recreation of the legendary dish of Kings. Woodcock stuffed in pigeon, stuffed in partridge, stuffed in pheasant, stuffed in... Was he interested? Odilio swatted her away. He felt like throwing up. Waiting outside his editor's office, the sack was starting to feel like an inevitability. Odilio was rehearsing how he'd break the news to his wife.

Cooper Martin, The Gent's editor and an industry giant, poked his head out of the room and called Odilio inside. Cooper ran a tight ship at the magazine, but there was a warmth to him that came through in person. Never taking himself too seriously, he had a knack for seeing things from differing points of view and making editorial decisions drawing on a pool of feedback. A large man of seventy, with a head of thick white hair, he'd worked in the industry since his early twenties.

He knew everything there was to know about magazines. He'd watched the world change over the years — had seen the industry rise and fall — yet never seemed fazed by any of it. As a teenager, he'd been a great squash player, almost choosing the path of the sportsman over journalism, until a ligament injury put the matter to bed for him. At times, Odilio supposed his boss's durability lay in a slight detachment from work. The magazine was a job, and that's all it was to him.

"Everything seems to be ticking along," said Cooper, adjusting himself in his chair. "I thought your last piece, the GALAXIAS one, was good. Really good, actually. Are you happy here?"

"I am," said Odilio, forcing a smile.

"It sounds like you've got some interesting projects lined up. Amy was telling me about this new book. Stuffing birds? Sounds very up your street."

"So I'm told," said Odilio, forcing another awkward smile.

"Well, there are no plans to change what we're doing here. I'm sure you read the monthly reports: sales are okay — the shareholders are happy, for now. I can't pay anyone more than what they're on, I've said that to everyone. I'm sure it's not a problem for you, of course. How is Helena?" A glum expression quickly found its way to Odilio's face. Relief was turning to frustration. He looked at Cooper. His editor's eyes, when sufficiently focused, were like the eyes of a hawk — the sharpest features in an otherwise round head.

"What's wrong?" Cooper asked.

"It's silly," said Odilio.

"You can tell me. You know I can't stand an unhappy employee."

"It's stupid, in fact, but it's on my mind."

"Then tell me," said Cooper, rubbing his hands together. "Nothing leaves these four walls."

Odilio checked around to see if anyone was listening. "I think people hate me," he said.

Cooper stared at him, his expression unchanging.

"I got on Twitter recently. It's stupid, but I've been reading the comments — it's horrible what people are saying. It's ruining my work."

Cooper furrowed his eyebrows. "I'm listening," he said.

"It's making me question what the point of all this is. I know I rubbed people up the wrong way, but I didn't think I was that bad. They hate me and I don't know what to do."

Cooper cleared his throat. "What sort of things?"

"What do you mean?"

"What are they calling you?"

"Oh." Odilio pulled out his phone, glancing at Cooper before his eyes found the Twitter feed. "Well, for instance: 'Odilio is a miserable old bastard with nothing decent to say ever.'" He scrolled down. "'I would sooner pull out my teeth than read the inane ramblings of The Gent's in-house misanthrope, Odilio Brimble.'" He looked at Cooper again. "This one's a bit nastier," he said. "'A useless gammon with a public school accent. Wouldn't hesitate running the twat over if I saw him in the street' — that gives you a good idea, really. I get called gammon a lot." He slipped his phone back into his pocket. "I'm not even that red," he added, stroking the side of his face.

"You know, it's not my first time hearing this?" Cooper popped his knuckles together. "A few writers of ours have gone offline recently — Tom in the motors section and Michael in suits. It's not their fault people are dreadful." He stretched out his arms. "What I've told them is this: think of the internet like a real net — a net for catching sharks in. It's a good analogy if you'll hear it out. Now, most of the fish in the sea are normal fish, like you and me — they mind their own business, they swim through the gaps in the net. But the sharks — the ones that get trapped — they're the losers who spend all day online, writing crap for everyone else to read. Do you understand what I'm saying?" Odilio nodded, but he did not understand. He wondered if Cooper was making the analogy up on the spot. "Now, it's this small group of losers, the ones writing nasty things, the sharks who can't escape the net, who end up getting the attention of the rest of us. I don't know anyone who used the internet to reach out to someone that inspired them. I bet you don't, either. Your favourite musicians, writers, filmmakers: they're all out there waiting to be contacted, but I bet you've never bothered to say one nice thing to them ever."

"It's true," said Odilio. "I haven't."

"Of course, you haven't! Our readers have got better things to do than fart about on Twitter, am I right?"

"Quite," said Odilio. He wished the same was true of himself.

"Here," said Cooper, standing up to browse his bookshelf. "I don't let many people into this, but I keep tabs on all my writers. I keep a collection of their best work." He nudged a footstool into position, stood on it and reached for a box on the highest shelf. He lifted it down to the desk, blew the dust off the lid, and then spread its contents over the table.

Nothing attests to the passing of time as honestly as paper, Odilio thought, staring at the collection of newspapers before him. It surprised him to see those early editions of his work so visibly aged: the paper had wrinkled, warped like corrugated iron from cycles of dry and damp, jaundiced by oxidation. "Wow," he remarked, picking up a 1997 edition of The Sunday Times. "I haven't seen these in years."

Cooper grinned. "Let's fix some drinks and have a read. Scotch?"

"Please," said Odilio. Cooper rummaged through his spirit cabinet, as Odilio glanced at the headline: 'Greek Twist: Making A Right Mezze Of Things'. His eyes scanned the column beneath a youthful-looking image of him. He began reading:

'With a twist' — that most insipid and uninspiring of phrases. Only a stiff martini is tolerable with a twist (of lime, never lemon, thank you). Nothing else is worth condemning to the inevitable disappointment. It's one thing to do something badly — over time, such things can be fixed. But the outlook for a restaurateur who champions 'with a twist' is frankly more terminal. Only a serious detachment from reality could lead someone to consider an English take on Greek cuisine a good

idea. 'Fusion food' — another phrase that gets my pulse going for all the wrong reasons…

Odilio's eyes skipped a few paragraphs.

Greek Twist is co-owned by Amy Reeds of Surrey and Dimitri Kappas of Greece. One gets the sense it's Amy who wears the toga here. It's difficult to imagine that archetype of Mediterranean machismo, Alexis Zorba, ordering the vegetarian souvlaki with English spring vegetables where the lamb should be. Still, buggery has a long tradition in Grecian culture, continued here by Greek Twist, just off the Edgware Road…

Odilio put the paper down with a grin. "Blast," said Cooper, looking up from the cabinet. "We're out of scotch — I only have this bottle of vermouth."

"Then two glasses of vermouth," Odilio smiled.

"Unorthodox," said Cooper, pouring two large glasses. He brought them over to the desk and handed one to Odilio. They cheersed and took a drink. "How are you getting on?" Cooper asked. "Good stuff ey?"

"The vermouth or my articles? This vermouth is rancid," Odilio laughed.

"Ah, but the articles are brilliant. I respected your work long before you worked here. I knew we'd have you someday."

"They were good times," Odilio said wistfully. The job had been a hell of a lot more fun back then. Reading his old columns stirred a mixture of feelings in him. In those pages was a quality of his younger self: a voice, a syntactical blueprint that was waking something aged in its absence.

"Let's have a look," Cooper said, taking one from the pile. "1994, Jesus: some of my hairs still had colour back then. Ah, this one's brilliant: your review of Seppa. I remember you getting first access. Actually, we were livid you got the scoop." Cooper put the paper down on the table. Odilio picked it up to read.

We file into the dining room of Seppa with the solemnity of German POWs on the Eastern Front. There is one question on our minds: can Tony Romano replicate his three Michelin star success at Porco? Or will his new baby, in a quiet corner of Fitzrovia, fail to live up to the gargantuan hype? It doesn't take long to receive our answer. The mood lifts almost at once, crescendoing into the most almighty of celebrations only a character like Mr Romano could create.

Odilio remembered that night fondly. His friend, the charismatic and talented chef, Tony Romano, was launching his second restaurant and had invited the upstarting Odilio (and fifty others) to the opening party. What a night it had been. The dinner had succeeded in every expectation. Odilio could still taste the roast partridge, served (with only the confidence of a world-class chef) alongside a solitary prune. Tony must have known rave reviews would follow that night; he'd finished it dancing on the tables, pouring limoncello into the mouths of his hysterically-entertained and well-fed guests.

This was the beginning of his relationship with Tony. Years later, they'd co-presented 'The Critic and The Cook', touring Britain's restaurants, exploring the nation's grapple with modernising gastronomy — admonishing the failures, trumpeting the successes that had broken ranks into modernity. They'd filmed three seasons throughout the noughties. The show had done well in Britain, but Tony,

22

hungry for trans-Atlantic success, had gone on to try his luck in America. Odilio hadn't joined.

"You're smiling," said Cooper, raising his glass. "See, isn't it good once in a while to remind yourself who you are? I know writers hate looking back at their work, but it's important to do so. It helps figure out where you're going."

Odilio nodded. "You're right, Cooper, thank you."

"Everyone's so busy fitting in nowadays," his editor continued. "You need to stop worrying about what people think. They read your column because they crave a spectacle. Your opinion — your unrestrained opinion — that is the spectacle. And look, it hasn't worked out badly for your friend Tony."

Cooper was right. In America, Tony had found success through an increasingly played-up version of himself. His bolshie, no-fucks-given attitude was the thrust of his appeal. There was no shortage of detractors, but Tony Romano was the last person on earth who paid them any attention. It was an attitude Odilio had long wished to reestablish himself.

"I've got an idea," said Cooper, finishing off his glass. "Christ, that was horrible, I'll get some proper stuff next time." He put the glass down on the table with a bang. "Anyway, I've got an idea. To get you back in your stead: get your old voice back."

"I'm all ears."

"Nice easy hit piece. You can go for it, all guns blazing."

"Please."

"The Lancaster. It's reopening next week. Matthew Watts as head chef: the next prospect of vegan cuisine. In my opinion, a jumped-up nerd with anger issues. How about it?"

Odilio smiled at his editor. "It's perfect, Cooper," he said.

4

Tabitha was in the middle of a tutorial when Odilio burst into the room with two sacks of groceries. "Good evening," he said with an excitable, mischievous air about him. With its default white interiors, the dining room was the room of the house that contained the fewest furnishings. The long glass table in the middle lent it all the cosiness of a sanatorium. A solitary artwork decorated the far wall. A giant piece of paper was finished off with a scribble of charcoal and suspended in a more impressive frame. Little else in the vast space had it feeling like a home. Indeed, the room seemed built for a larger scale of people.

"Ah, Stuart, you're here." He was getting used to the tutor's presence in the house. Conscious of the impending Common Entrance exams (now less than four years away), Helena had decided on a private tutor for Tabitha, who had just started year five. There were suspicions Tabitha might be dyslexic — a view her teachers failed to share — and so the testimony of a private tutor could lend credibility to this hunch. Odilio had reminded his wife that it was with maths that Tabitha struggled, so Helena had extended her diagnosis to include dyscalculia and a potential attention deficit disorder. Stuart came four evenings a week, Monday to Friday (with a day off on Wednesday). Whenever Odilio interrupted their classes, he found them in the same place, working through whatever they did together. That Tabitha could sit still for such long periods was progress enough in his eyes. Previous tutors had suffered terribly from Tabitha's excitable moods, although

Helena and Odilio secretly agreed it was their fault for failing to leverage the appropriate discipline with her. Even the au pair, Rachel, they agreed, was overly reluctant to challenge Tabitha's boisterousness, indulging her more often than was healthy. In their nine years raising Tabitha, they'd never come across a sufficiently authoritative child carer. Odilio had started to wonder if it was a fundamental contradiction in the temperament attracted to such a line of work.

"How is my little Tabby cat doing?" Odilio cooed. Tabitha had been reading aloud from her book and had stopped as soon as her father entered.

"I'm good," she said, her eyes fixed on the table. Stuart sat opposite her and acknowledged Odilio with a quick dip of his head. The tutor had made a solid impression in his interview. At length, he'd discussed the benefits of a holistic education encompassing a playful approach to learning while appreciating the need to get their daughter into the best school possible. On meeting Tabitha, opening their conversation with talk of a computer game Odilio was only vaguely familiar with — was it Minecraft? RoadBlocks? — the tutor had sealed the deal. He'd even hit it off with the au pair, Rachel, who being around his age, encouraged the view in Helena they should become close friends. On Stuart, the family was sold. Odilio had no good reason to say anything otherwise. Since arriving at the house, Odilio had hardly paid the tutor attention. All week, his thoughts were on the meeting with Cooper. All week, he'd passed through the motions on auto-pilot.

Now, Odilio studied the tutor's face. He had strong features like an Easter Island head. His dark brown hair was tied back in a ponytail, and he had a substantial beard of the same colour. Despite all the hair, he had a young face and

26

looked in his mid-twenties. Only his dress sense let him down. Frayed cargo trousers, a loose, unironed shirt, and running shoes gave him the appearance of a young geography professor. The intellectual middle classes believed a lacking style could be compensated with good conversation. How wrong they were, Odilio thought. A smart, well-fitting outfit did more to make a solid impression than a hundred clever exchanges.

"What are you reading?" Odilio wandered over.

"It's called The Little Boy from Aleppo," Tabitha held up her book.

"Any good?" Odilio smiled and put down the groceries on the table.

"It's very good, actually," said Tabitha. "It's about a boy who moves to England—"

"From Aleppo?"

Tabitha nodded. "Yes, and it's about the mean children at his school, but they don't know what he's been through."

"Would he rather be in Aleppo?"

Tabitha looked at the book. "Erm, no," she said. "Not really. Because he can't and he just wants the children to be nicer to him. He does have one friend, though."

"Good for the boy from Aleppo," Odilio chuckled. "How is she doing?" Odilio addressed the tutor.

"Very well," said Stuart.

"Excellent. Well, I'm about to start on dinner. Are you interested in sticking around for something?"

"That's very kind," said the tutor, "but I'll have to shoot after this."

"Are you sure? We're having roast pigeon. It's a family speciality."

"Sounds delicious but I'm vegan, I should confess. I'd be no use."

"Vegan?" Odilio snorted. "Well, you've come to the wrong house, haven't you?" He winked at the tutor. "Suit yourself, I better leave you to it." He picked up his bags, whistling as he left the room.

Odilio removed his scarf and jacket and hung them over a stool. He emptied the bags onto the kitchen island. On his way back from the office, he'd picked up some bits from the grocer, including a good red, which he uncorked, letting it breathe as he browsed the news on his phone. He was chipper this evening; chirpy. He'd give their cook the night off and prepare something exquisite for his family. Hunched over the kitchen island, he got to work, gutting and defeathering the pigeons, slicing the onions to set the base for a jus. After peeling the potatoes, he ran them under water to remove the excess starch. When Odilio was in a good mood, cooking was the perfect outlet to share his love with other people.

Within minutes, the room had filled with the smell of wine and herbs. The crimson jus bubbled on a gentle simmer. After parboiling the potatoes, Odilio sliced and prepared them in cream to bake in the oven a la dauphinoise. He butchered the pigeons with the same precise knife movements he'd picked up from his father. A jolt of nostalgia overcame him as he removed the breasts. Odilio's father passed away when Odilio was eighteen. From time to time, it dawned on him he was unable to recall his voice anymore. Only occasionally did it come back to him as a flicker of memory, either in dreams or in moments like this.

28

Odilio's grandfather had been the head of the Galloway hunt. Famed for his extravagant tastes, his huge parties and hedonistic tendencies were the stuff of legend. But his grandfather had been a fool with his money. He held the parties on credit, pissing a fortune away on scotch and champagne. With no way of paying his debts, he declared bankruptcy and died a year later, hauled up in the estate in Dumfries (later repossessed by his creditors). Odilio's parents had to work hard. His father, who had begun adulthood with the moneyed ambition of becoming an actor, found work at a freight company on the Scottish west coast. Odilio's mother taught at the local school. They took out loans to send their son to Eton, but there was hope again for the future of the Brimbles. Odilio had taken to public school like a fish in water. Something in his blood remembered the way things had been. His Scottish burr left him in a week; he never looked back. After Eton, there was Oxford, and after Oxford, there was the high society of London. In Helena, the beautiful aristocrat, who blended the old and new with elegance and grace, he found final affirmation of his return to the upper echelons.

But Odilio's father never got over the loss of the prestige he'd grown up with. Back-breaking work at the freight company didn't make it easier, either. Odilio fled the nest and his old man packed it in. Dead at forty-nine. Massive heart attack. Odilio's mother died several years later from a vicious and rapidly proliferating cancer, just as Odilio's career was beginning to take off. It was all so long ago, Odilio had started to consider himself an orphan of sorts. Slicing up the pigeons, preparing a herb rub, he felt a bittersweet joy in making this old family favourite. His parents loved food. His father retained the hunting habits of his old

29

man, albeit without the pomp and prestige of those earlier Galloway ceremonies. As a boy, Odilio had learnt to shoot game birds: how to defeather, gut, and butcher them properly. He'd learnt to fish when he was younger than Tabitha, and he'd taken to cooking from his mother, watching her prepare the fruits of the day's labour in their kitchen with naturality and love he cherished to this day. This was the foundation of his culinary passion.

How could he let his parents down? Odilio thought, swirling the good red and sipping it slowly. How dare he complain, living so well off the fruits of their hard work? They'd broken themselves for him: they'd sacrificed their lives so he could chase his dreams. Odilio thought back to the conversation with Cooper. His editor was right: it was time to get a grip. Every successful person at some point becomes disenfranchised by their success. They normalise it and take it for granted, it having become everything they know. Well, it was time to take it seriously again. And The Lancaster — what a fantastic opportunity for a comeback. He would write a piece they would talk about for years to come.

Odilio put the pigeons in the oven and set the timer. He had enough time for a quick visit to his study and poured himself more wine as an accompaniment. Soon he was on Twitter, scanning the comments on his GALAXIAS piece. Odilio didn't feel the usual anxiety browsing his feed. His experience at that restaurant had been truly dreadful. GALAXIAS was a monument to the tacky oligarchy that had infiltrated London in recent years. The night Odilio dined there, a famous MMA fighter was celebrating his birthday at the adjacent table. Odilio had watched with morbid curiosity as the head chef appeared from the kitchen to slice up a massive 20 lb beef brisket with a samurai sword whilst the MMA fighter and his friends spectated this procedure through their forever-recording phone screens. Why should Odilio let such perversions slide when he was supposed to be a bastion of food culture — someone who ensured that the craft of restauranteering was maintained to the highest standards possible? He needed to remind himself of his mandate as often as necessary. Restaurant critics weren't crowd-pleasers: it was their job to tell the Emperor everyone could see his arse.

@thefinnegan1: 'Went galaxias with the missus for her birthday. Good view of the london eye. Don't listen to this twat.'

Odilio clicked 'reply'. Without thinking, he typed: 'Good view of the worst attraction in London? It's fitting that your horizons stretch so far.' He hesitated and pressed 'enter'. A giddy rush of excitement overcame him. He closed Twitter and shut the laptop. Time to bite back, he thought, staring at the wall. Time to stop being so passive. Above, the taxidermied head of a gurning boar looked back at him. The other heads adorning the study were from exotic animals won by his grandfather on various trips to Africa. The boar was the single contribution of his father. Odilio had been in attendance for the kill one Easter holiday in France. His father had stuffed it himself. Odilio liked the angry, confused look etched across the creature's face. It was better than having it appear placid, serene — contented with its status as wall furniture. Even in death, the boar retorted with its look. It made the conquest all the more sweeter. Odilio fancied a similar approach to his trolls: hanging their heads on the wall like slaughtered quarry as they gnashed, spat, and

31

cursed his name. The timer alarm sounded: the pigeon was finished. Odilio raced

back to the kitchen, his stomach gurgling in anticipation of the roasted flesh.

5

"Cheers," said Helena, holding up her glass to toast Elias's gimlet. He mumbled something in reply, scanning the crowded bar as if looking for someone he knew. "To your certain and well-deserved success," she added, noticing that he was sweating heavily. Elias Karlsson was the only child of her most loyal customer, Ingrid. The matriarch of a Swedish noble family she'd sold millions of pounds worth of art to over the years. Now, she counted Ingrid's son as her protege: a young artist she would mentor, mould, and promote. An act of generosity, first and foremost. She knew very well of the stresses he'd put his poor mother through back in Malmö, and now she was doing her bit to keep him out of trouble. It was a good deed that could pay off in more ways than one. Helena was testing a long-held theory that anything could make money if managed correctly.

Elias was wondering whether it would be inappropriate to do some cocaine in the toilet. A little something to take the edge off. Why was it so hot in here, he wondered? He sipped his gimlet, which was bitter and strong, then surveyed the room, doing his best to make his distractedness seem like it had an artistic basis to it. His intentions were pretty straightforward: he wanted the woman opposite him to think he was observing something in the atmosphere otherwise elusive to her. Something only perceptible to a sensitive and artistic soul such as his own. A bit of coke would take the edge off. Why was it so hot in here? He wiped his forehead with his jacket sleeve then sipped his drink again. Heat stifled him. He acted unnaturally when it was hot. What else could explain his unnaturalness around her? Why were his usual insights unable to flow? He'd be lucky if she didn't already think him a total simpleton. Elias Karlsson, rising star conceptual artist, at thirty-two years old, felt like a nervous schoolboy again.

"The new piece is terrific," Helena said, her gaze fixed on the artist. His round spectacles magnified his eyes like a cartoon character. His curly blonde hair was so voluminous it looked permed. Helena was thinking: the beret would have to go when they were more familiar, as would the other signifiers of his outgrown adolescence. Leather was back in, so he could keep the jacket, but the faded Ninja Turtle t-shirt was unforgivable on a man his age, *especially* when worn ironically. She watched as he fidgeted in his chair, his eyes on anything but her. She spoke in a friendly tone to help him relax, but it seemed to have the opposite effect. He would need to be trained to court the approval of braying socialites if he wanted to be successful in the arse-kissing world of modern art.

The waiter came and Elias ordered another gimlet. Helena opted for a small glass of white wine. "I want to start exhibiting your work next year," she said, as their drinks arrived. She leaned forward. "I'm going to announce an exclusive pre-exhibition auction, buy up before you blow up, sort of thing." Elias nodded. "People like to get in early. You sell more, and for higher, at these little events than you ever do at the main calendar auctions. Your long-term investors will come out and they'll support you down the line whatever you do — makes sense for their investments, right? I want the exhibition somewhere off the beaten track. A location with a bit of edge: Berlin, maybe. Something to keep you exciting with the London crowd. The auction will shift your larger, portfolio-friendly pieces. I'll announce something to my list next week, does that sound good to you?" Elias nodded again.

"We're going to run with the Hearts series," Helena said, leaning back in her chair. It was the first complete series of work he'd produced after failing his design degree in Stockholm and turning his hand to art. Her private belief was that he hadn't done anything better since. He'd gained a certain intellectual credibility over the years, but as is often the way with the young artist, he'd struggled to develop his work such that it pooled from a deeper part of him.

"It has the best commercial appeal," Helena continued. "It's accessible; the themes are universal. It's also your most complete collection, with some durable items that investors will be comfortable lending. We don't want everything snapped up and stored in vaults for years. The work will have to get out via its backers, so we want to encourage that as best as we can. As the proud owner of the centrepiece of the Hearts collection, I can honestly say they'll be fighting to get their hands on your work."

Elias blushed as they cheersed again. "I'm going to the toilet," he announced.

6

At twenty-nine, most of Rachel's friends had 'real' jobs and long-term partners: the makings of mortgage deposits tucked into joint savings accounts. Her schoolmates from Devonshire — an even wealthier cohort than her university friends — owned their own houses, helped in every case by their parents. Rachel felt behind in life when she took stock of such details. She rented a room in a house share for a considerable portion of her income. Her savings couldn't secure the downpayment on a car loan. She had no pets or partner — only a few house plants gave her any sense of responsibility. She was the au pair for a wealthy family for whom she worked six evenings a week while her friends met at fancy bars after a hard day's work. She assisted a nine-year-old in such tasks as completing their homework and taking a bath whilst explaining to anyone who'd listen how her ambition to become a children's illustrator was going as well as it could.

"Let's play hide and seek," Tabitha asked for a third time. She was in a restless mood. Most evenings, Tabitha was allowed half an hour of games and usually wanted nothing more than to play on her father's iPad. It was a preference Rachel tried to discourage in her: she did her best to make the more traditional, imagination-based games as exciting as possible. Yet here she was, tapping away at her phone, distracted by the same technology she tried to dismiss as uninteresting. "I want to play hide and seek," Tabitha winged, pulling on Rachel's arm.

"For dinner?" Maria, the house cook, asked, appearing at the sitting room doorway.

"Oh, yes, please," said Rachel, glancing up from her phone. She would eat something and then get Tabitha to bed; there would be time to make the drinks at a friend's house on the other side of London.

"What you like?" asked Maria.

"What are we having?" Rachel asked Tabitha. "I'm starving."

Maria had been head-hunted by Helena on a family holiday to Crete. Originally from Bulgaria, she was the head chef of a restaurant popular with the island's yachting classes. Her food had been simple, healthy, and delicious; Maria was offered the job over dessert, with a promise to receive double whatever the restaurant was paying her. It spoke to a general tendency of Helena's: a belief in her power to make brilliant, split-second decisions, from everything to the staff she employed to her dabblings in the art world. Odilio called it impulsiveness, but so far, it hadn't let them down. Maria was further evidence for this self-assurance. She'd been with the family for six years — was still learning English — and had a habit of abbreviating sentences in a way that was a sort of code among the family.

"You know, I'd love some of those chicken dumplings," said Rachel. "Tabby, they were delicious, weren't they?"

Tabitha frowned and stuck out her tongue. "I don't want to eat chicken," she said.

"But you love chicken," said Rachel.

Tabitha folded her arms. "Stuart says they kill them when they're alive. I'm not eating chicken anymore."

"But chicken very good," said Maria.

Odilio entered the living room, skirting past Maria in the doorway, taking a seat on the sofa next to Tabitha. "What's everyone up to?" he smiled.

"We're debating dinner," said Rachel.

"Oh, *dinner*," said Odilio, studying his daughter's expression.

"Tabs says she won't eat chicken."

"No chicken," said Maria.

"No chicken!" said Odilio with mock outrage. He brushed a hand through his hair.

Initially, he'd failed to warm to Maria. Although his wife usually made the staff selections (she spent more time in the house was the winning argument), there was a clear case for him to choose their chef based on the fact that judging people's cooking was the essence of his trade. The argument didn't get him far. Helena conceded any restaurant visit was in the remit of Odilio's decision, but the house cook was a health practitioner first and foremost. They would not live to ninety in good health, eating the food Odilio made a living fawning over. The matter was settled, and Maria was hired. Only in recent years had Odilio seen sense in his wife's choice. Maria was adaptable and competent, but best of all, she was good at blending into the house environment: there when you needed her and gone when you did not.

"So what would Queen Tabitha like to eat?" asked Odilio.

38

Tabitha shrugged her shoulders. "I don't want to eat animals," she said. "I don't want to eat cows, either. I don't want to eat lions or rhinoseus."

"Rhinoceroses," Rachel corrected, glancing at Odilio. "But no one eats those."

"Good," said Tabitha. "And I don't want to eat chicken."

"What about pork?" Odilio asked.

Tabitha thought for a second. "No," she said.

Odilio leaned forward. "Why not? Is it an animal?"

She hesitated before saying: "Yes."

"Pork is an animal? I've never heard of a pork. Have you, Rachel? What does a pork look like? What sound does the pork make?"

"No idea," Rachel grinned.

"It's got a tail," said Tabitha.

"Really?" said Odilio.

Tabitha nodded. "And big eyes and horns."

Odilio winked at Maria, who understood nothing. "I'll let you decide what you want, but I'm having my own delicious dinner. Maria, could you make a carbonara?"

"Oh, yes," said Rachel.

"You're staying for dinner?"

"Please," she said.

"Make a big one," said Odilio. "Car-bo-na-ra," he rearticulated to her.

"I want carbonara, too," said Tabitha.

Odilio chuckled as he left the room.

7

The restaurant at The Lancaster Hotel is one of the oldest fine-dining establishments in London. An early importer of classic French cuisine to the city, it has changed hands a dozen times in the last century, each time seemingly to outdo itself in the extent of its deterioration (most recently, as an American-style BBQ 'bistro', it had become synonymous with a culinary fall from grace). Whispers of a comeback have followed The Lancaster around like a bad smell since its heyday, but the announcement that a Michelin-star chef would reinvent the place from scratch was met with enthusiasm in the industry. When Matthew Watts was named the architect of this overhaul, the news polarised chefs and critics alike.

The taxi pulled into the mews opposite the restaurant. With its stone portico and Christmas-cake embellishments cracked and peeling on the greying facade, the tired look of the old place still lingered. Odilio knocked on the door. A smartly dressed man in his early thirties opened and introduced himself as The Lancaster's head of PR. He escorted Odilio through the main dining room — revamped in an industrial-minimal aesthetic incongruous to the exterior (hideous as far as Odilio was concerned; he made a mental note) — on to a small office at the back, where Matthew Watts was waiting at his desk.

Matthew Watts was not your typical rising star chef. The thirty-seven-year-old Bristolean wore his ginger hair in spindly dreadlocks. He had a sensitive air about him, Odilio thought. With his skinny build and pale pallor, there was something fragile about him. Most of the chefs Odilio knew carried themselves with the physical menace of cage fighters. It was not sensitive work. You needed to be tough in the kitchen. The challenge for the young upstart was not just to survive but to thrive: to satisfy the commands of your superiors, whilst trying to get one over the others bustling for a seat at the top. It was not enough to defend, you had to be on the offensive at all times. Odilio knew many great cooks, but only a few who could hack the kitchen environment to go on to become great chefs.

"A pleasure to meet you," said Odilio as he entered the office. Matthew Watts rose from his desk, reached out and shook Odilio's hand.

"Likewise," he said, inviting Odilio to a pair of beanbags on the floor. "We'll be more comfortable on those." Odilio lowered himself onto the orange one. He glanced at the bookshelf next to him: his eyes caught volumes on Qigong and Zen meditation. The chef sat on the beanbag opposite as the PR agent poured two glasses of sparkling water. The Lancaster was going in a drastically new direction: reconstructed, as Matthew Watts had done with success elsewhere, as a gluten-free, vegan gastro-restaurant. Odilio knew there would be suspicions over his motives for an interview. He detected defensiveness in the air. At the same time, he knew they had a puncher's chance going against England's most prolific meat eater the week before their launch. If Odilio didn't nail it perfectly, he could come across as sloppy and washed-up. It would confirm everything his detractors were saying. But, this evening, Odilio was in the zone. Cooper's words were alive in him, as was the memory of his father, grandfather, his mother, and all the Brimbles before them who knew you had to be calm before you took your shot.

"I assume you've got your questions prepared. We can dive in right away," Matthew Watts said, monotonously. "I'm happy for you to use a recording device." Odilio placed his phone next to his notebook on the floor and turned the recorder on. There were the usual warm-up questions: What was his vision for The Lancaster? Where did he get his inspiration from? What did he hope to do differently from his seemingly cursed predecessors? This was the cud-chewing stage of the interview, where they fattened you with nutritionless filler — dead publicity-isms that would rarely make the final cut. Matthew Watts spoke at length about bio-hydraulic crop cycles, sustainable inter-foraging, rewilding and a host of buzzwords that were just short of banned from the pages of The Gent. Odilio listened with palpable disinterest. The scrawny chef was indefatigable when it came to rattling off his opinions — Odilio soon felt smothered listening to them all. Self-awareness seemed distinctly lacking within the redecorated walls of The Lancaster. Did they really believe they were going to fill The Gent's pages with this twaddle?

"We've basically abandoned the idea of menuing," the chef said, readjusting his spectacles. His habit of verbifying random nouns irritated Odilio, who made a note in his book. "Menus set a capitalist precedent. It's like, if I'm putting artichokes on, I'm saying I can guarantee them. But, of course, to do that I'm going to have to exploit someone. I mean, artichokes aren't always in season. I can't claim to have good ones every day. So I have to draw a line and say, look, this is an unsustainable precedent. We're going to serve what we've got and what's good. Good for the planet as well."

Odilio knew his readership well. The British public resented being lectured to. They'd disparage anyone, no matter their level of expertise, if they felt they were being looked down on. Odilio would get under the chef's skin by playing stupid. Lure him in with his cluelessness. Trip him up with feigned confusion so as to gaslight his convictions.

"So what has climate change got to do with food?" Odilio said, in response to a long-winded passage about the comparative methane emissions of different grain-based milks. Matthew Watts shot him a confused look. "We're talking about the heat retenance of carbon bonds in the stratosphere."

"I know," said Odilio. "But you've used so many big words, I can't keep up. Let me make a quick note. Climate change: it's bad, right?"

"Yes…" The chef stroked his beard. "Now, I was saying that cashew nut shell liquid has been shown to decrease enteric methane emissions. So, it's like, should we *encourage* its use? I like the idea, if we're going to run an evolving menu, then the selection should be based on what Gaia wants, too — you know, what's good for the earth."

"Would you do a burger if someone wanted it?"

"We do 'do a burger'," the chef said.

"A proper beef one, if someone really wanted it?"

The chef studied Odilio. "I've told you, we're meat-free."

"Yes, but what if I stuffed a thousand pounds in your pocket — would it be something you'd consider then?"

Matthew Watts shook his head. "What are you getting at? A thousand pounds to discredit everything we've worked towards? Of course I wouldn't."

"Implying there's a price?"

"In theory, as a one-off… I'd reinvest the money, of course. Anyway, let's move on. Any other questions?"

Odilio looked at his notebook. "What is gluten and why is he so bad?"

The chef leaned back into the bean bag, realising he was being had. He shrugged and gave Odilio a pitying look. "I think we're finished here."

"No, no, I'm sorry," said Odilio. "One final question, I promise I'll be quick." This was the stuff resurrections were made of, he thought. He could already see the delighted look on Cooper's face. Matthew Watts raised an eyebrow as Odilio cleared his throat. "What would you say to the reader who thought this was all pseudo-scientific claptrap: that by using new-age vocabulary and the atmosphere of cloying, self-love consumerism you've created an ideological anaesthetic for the same capitalist excesses practised elsewhere?"

The chef stared at him, his eyes like those of a lizard. It was a hate-filled look — the sort of look caused by the suppression of a violent reaction. Matthew Watts stood up. "Cunt," he muttered, before leaving the room. Odilio made a note in case it wasn't audible on the tape. He stopped recording.

The head of PR escorted him out the building. "I bet you're feeling very clever," he said as they made their way across the dining room. "We wanted to reach out to your readership — that was frankly pathetic of you."

Odilio shrugged. "You'll have to do better than that if you want their attention. It was supposed to be an interview, not a sermon."

"What a sad man you are, Mr Brimble. Men like you are so scared." The head of PR closed the door in his face. Odilio let out a hearty laugh, then skipped down the stairs onto the street.

The assignment had gone as well as he could have hoped for, he thought in the back of the taxi. Now, his plan was simple. He would get home and fortify himself in his study with a drink. Throw himself into his work while the ideas were fresh. Before dawn, he'd have a brand-spanking piece of copy to send his editor's way. He sank into his seat as his mind poured over details of the evening, committing his thoughts to paper as he did.

His phone beeped as the taxi made its way through Belgravia. He had one new message from 'Matthew (Lancaster)'. An apology? Round two? Odilio waited nervously for the text to load.

Just saw the news about your mate, Tony. Have fun explaining that to everyone you obsolete piece of shit.

8

Odilio raced to his room. He shut the study door and switched on the emeralite lamp before opening his laptop. His legs shot up and down like pistons as he typed 'Tony Romano' into Google, mistyping it several times in his hurry. Breaking news confirmed his fears: a dozen headlines stood out as a jumble of words he was slow to make sense of. He forced himself to read each line, one at a time. 'Sex Shame Chef: Tony Romano FILMED Harassing Waitress'; 'Racism and Misogyny in Tony Romano's Kitchen', and: 'All The Sexual Harassment Allegations Against Tony Romano So Far'. Looking back at this moment, he would observe how quickly he'd understood — that perhaps he'd already understood in the car, reading the text from Matthew. And yet he'd never craved clarity as much as he did now. A power cut at that moment could have induced an aneurysm. He clicked the first article on the BBC news and started reading:

A wave of sexual harassment allegations against Tony Romano have come to light following a leaked recording of the British-Italian chef as he begins filming his new series for Sky...

Tony was in London filming 'Go Hard or Go Rome' — this, Odilio knew. Not content with running the best Italian restaurants in the world, Tony had branched out into television, first on 'The Critic and The Cook' with Odilio, he'd since played a larger-than-life version of himself on several TV shows, spanning four continents, culminating in this latest series that saw him help struggling Italian restaurants turn a profit. From Wakefield to Weymouth, he toured the country, lending a hand to his brethren who dreamed of running high-quality establishments themselves (although the show's entertaining thrust came from those restaurateurs who were beyond helping). On top of this, Tony had made a fortune with his grocery and cooking utensil line, Romano & Rome. He still owned his original Michelin-star establishments, Seppa and Porco, but he'd bulked these out by turning them into a mediocre but profitable restaurant chain.

The leaked recording came a few paragraphs later. Odilio clicked 'play'. In the video Tony Romano is chatting to a group of male chefs about one of the restaurant's waitresses. "Uptight little cow, isn't she?" he can be heard saying. "Is she always like this?" There's a mild ascent of laughter from the others. "Usually," says someone, off camera. Tony mutters something under his breath. The waitress returns and, ignoring the men, reaches down to the dry cupboard for something. With her back turned, Tony takes the opportunity to make a thrusting gesture at her. The men laugh; the young woman, realising what's happening, quickly leaves the room. "Stuck-up bitch," Tony calls out to her. He turns to the only black member of the group, grins, and says: "Good back on her, though. You lot love de bottom." The video ends there.

Several women have since accused Mr Romano of similar behaviour. The women, all of whom worked with him at various points in his career, allege that sexual misconduct on the part of Mr Romano was rife in his working environment...

Looking back, Odilio would observe how straightforwardly he'd received the video's contents. Sitting in front of that screen, it did not feel like he was watching anyone other than the man he knew. That was Tony there. The effortless recognition transitioned seamlessly into sifting through more articles rather than disbelieving replays. This would only later register as the indictment it was.

Odilio checked Twitter. The hashtag: #TonyRomano was trending. Clicking the name brought him to the unfolding, live reactions of the site's hundreds of millions of users. It suddenly dawned on him: it was not the video or the tone of the allegations that inspired his building anxiety, but the relaying of these on a public forum that seemed to aggravate the swelling nausea inside him. Odilio was conscious he was breathing shallowly. He wanted a drink but couldn't bring himself to get up and fix one. The Twitter feed had achieved new heights to its salience. The past was being kicked up like settled scum; the waters of his mind were clouded with mud.

@Majik6616: 'Let's hope it's the end of the kitchen dinosaurs #TonyRomano.'

@BruceBunsin101: 'The cooking world is long overdue a #MeToo moment. First scalp is #TonyRomano.'

'I can attest this isn't a one-off incident,' someone had commented beneath a version of the video. 'I worked with Mr Romano back in 2006 at Seppa. He made several lewd remarks about my appearance all of which resulted in me quitting my job.'

'I was a waitress at Porco in the 90s,' someone else had said. 'Whenever I walked past Mr Romano in the kitchen, he would make a habit of groping me.'

'Dirty fucking pervert. I'll never forget him shoving his tongue down my throat while I was a runner on his show.'

Odilio had one notification. It was from @thefinnegan1, replying to his comment. Odilio clicked it and read. *Ahahahah at least I'm not best mates with a racist nonce.*

9

"I'm excited," said Helena, who was putting on foundation in front of the mirror. Odilio watched from the bed, alternating his attention between his phone and his wife, who liked to pepper in conversation to her frenzied ritual of getting dressed. "It's Elias's first auction. Well, his first proper one. He's nervous. I've told him not to be and that it's just a little thing." The tools of this twenty-minute process were strewn across the bedroom: the upturned jewellery boxes and discarded outfits called to mind the aftermath of a burglary. There were make-up items everywhere. Odilio's few possessions were arranged in a corner of the room: his pen, phone, and electric razor were laid out as if he was a guest for the night. The bedroom was one of the few rooms in the house visitors never saw: a room Helena made no effort to curate or keep tidy. Indeed, it took the flack for all the others: the fall-out for his wife's exhausting meticulousness was relinquished here.

"Just a little thing?" Odilio smirked. He knew no one with as large a social circle as Helena's. She could call on a hundred aristocrats with a day's notice, and almost all of them would show up.

Helena glanced at him in the mirror. "It's a Tuesday, darling. I sent the invitations on Sunday. I wouldn't exactly call it a headline auction." Odilio knew the secret by now. The trick was in the balance of the modest and the grand. Here was the modest: last-minute invitations to a small and intimate art auction held mid-week, made out as if she'd had the idea yesterday. Then there was the grand: the

£18,000 an evening West Room of the Savoy, with its unlimited bar and canapé kitchen. The wealth of the room would be in the order of hundreds of millions.

This is how it worked. You selected someone with a strong portfolio in the early stages of their career (a while out of art school — you needed someone with an established aesthetic who'd dropped the rock-the-boat radicalism of the graduate but who hadn't yet washed up). You assessed the strength of their portfolio on criteria such as its mass (bigger pieces were preferred by the more artistically illiterate investors; you needed work that could fill a large house). You selected a portfolio that was diverse, which the artist had a vision of expanding. Satisfied, you purchased a share of their collection as well as the rights to a portion of later work. Next, you promoted the artist to your circle, who paid an otherwise extortionate amount for the work of a 'nobody', but whose investment was fortified by the numbers. As the popularity grew, the value followed. All the artist had to do was keep a clean profile as you managed their output (you kept them motivated whilst observing the golden rule: investors never like an overly busy creator). A few years later, when the name had taken care of itself, you cashed in. Everyone was a winner, almost. It was a pyramid scheme, of course, lost by the last person not to turn a profit, but that was true for the sale of all art since the beginning of time. Somewhere down the line, even a Da Vinci would lose its unlucky owner their fortune.

"Oh, I do hope people show up," said Helena, putting on her earrings. "I'm worried I've left it too late. It would be humiliating to have a no-show."

"But everyone got back to you?" Odilio said, looking up from his phone.

"It means nothing until they're actually there. Oh, it would really hurt Elias if nobody turned up." Of course, they would show up, Odilio thought. In Elias, Helena had had a masterstroke. In representing a friend of the family, someone who hadn't developed a precociousness with so much as a limited success, she had found someone pliable, compliant, and ultimately cheap. None of that would hinder her from getting him to the top. But buying in now would be inexpensive compared to what he'd be worth later. People would come from all over to get a piece of the Elias pie. That was the cynical truth. The next step was dressing it up in a charade of artistic credibility.

"Darling, you're glued to your phone these days," Helena turned and peaked at his screen, catching the image of a familiar face. All week, Odilio had followed the story with obsessive detail. All week, one name had been on his mind and it was Tony's. His old friend had been sacked from his show and dropped by his sponsors. He'd been forced to resign as the CEO of his own company. Share prices had plummeted (that the company was his namesake didn't make it easy to sever the association). Odilio had savings tied up in Romano & Rome — what had been a lucrative investment for years suddenly turned to dust. Of course, Tony had broken every insider trading rule when he'd notified Odilio of the mergers and acquisitions taken by the company. He'd made his friends rich by taking these risks: Odilio was one of them. Now, it was all worthless. Odilio had received an email from his accountant just that morning. *What are we going to do?*

But the money wasn't the problem. Odilio had long accepted his wife as the family breadwinner. It embarrassed him to dwell on it too long. In the public eye, he represented upper-class excess. He loved playing up to the trope of the swaggering, pigeon-shooting gentleman: a man who took pride in having no idea what a pint of milk cost. "The best or tap water," he would remark when choosing the most expensive champagne on the menu. The truth was, he was no more than an accessory to the Courtney name. Like those tiny dogs French women carry in their handbags, he was simply a symptom of other people's wealth. Helena's parents described him as 'marrying in' (it was one of the reasons Helena hadn't changed her surname). To hear about his collapsed savings fund would only cement in their eyes his dependence on their money.

No, the money wasn't the problem — the swelling sense of shame was what was now eating him up. A fomenting sense of failure that threatened to destroy everything. Odilio could feel himself being sucked into a well of inertia. Tony was a dinosaur — he always had been. Odilio had seen this first hand on 'The Critic and The Cook'. His lechery was an open secret. Tony had tried it on with everyone, from the tea runner on work experience to the maître d' of the Ritz, he had a reputation for inappropriate advances and the bull-dozing of personal boundaries. It was all coming back to him. The drunken rowdiness, the bad behaviour in small-town hotels.... Why hadn't he said anything then?

Why hadn't he? The question ached him to consider. Dwelling on it only dredged up new memories — more data to stick the knife in. Looking back at those years was to witness his past turn into something ugly, as if a delicious banquet had suddenly disintegrated into a billion insects. A grotesque illusion. Something unnerved him, now, recollecting that past.

Odilio put the phone down on the bedside. "I was just checking my shares," he said.

"Well, let's not worry about those," said Helena, perched on the edge of the bed. "Have you spoken to him yet?"

"Not yet," Odilio shook his head.

"Well, when you do, I hope you tell him you're not in the slightest bit sorry for him. The man's a pig. I have zero sympathy."

"You're right," Odilio swallowed.

"He's never coming to this house again," Helena stood and kissed her husband on the forehead. "I hope you'll tell him that."

"I will," said Odilio, burrowing himself deeper into the sheets.

He was on Twitter as soon as Helena left the room. Now, new worries were beginning to take hold. Odilio feared the tarnishing of his own reputation as collateral for the destruction of Tony's. 'The Critic and The Cook' was a mainstay of noughties programming. Many considered the show Odilio's crowning achievement. Their two names were inseparable. Would the public assume complicity on his part? How good was it for anyone to have their name on the tip of the collective tongue when discussing a sexual predator?

Odilio only had to browse Twitter to rekindle his insecurities. 'I'd be interested to know what Odilio Brimble has to say about these allegations?' an old colleague at The Times had tweeted to 600 likes.

'Silence is violence on these issues,' someone had replied — a well-respected food writer who Odilio had met on several occasions and who he thoroughly liked.

'I reckon they're all at it,' chimed in someone else. Odilio's only Twitter comment was getting a string of replies: the single word 'nonce' had become something of a running joke as people echoed the sentiments of @thefinnegan1. Where could Odilio start? He put the phone back down and sighed, the familiar nausea thrumming around his gut.

10

"Elizabeth, you look fabulous," Helena beamed, taking two glasses of champagne from the table and passing one to her friend.

"You're looking pretty fab yourself," Elizabeth replied, checking Helena up and down. "Thank you," she took the champagne. "Coupe glasses — great touch," she added. "You hardly ever see these anymore."

"I can't stand flutes," said Helena, inspecting the shallow-bowled glass. "I feel like a frog — all neck and gullet — knocking it back from them. Odilio doesn't like them, either. His big nose gets in the way whenever he takes a sip." The two women burst out laughing.

"You know how they say the champagne glass is moulded on Marie Antoinette's breasts?" Elizabeth said. "I used to think they meant the flute glasses. I thought, poor Marie, breasts like stalactites, no wonder she was so rough on those serfs. It makes sense they were referring to these." They laughed again.

"Cheers," said Helena. "I'm so pleased you made it. You didn't have to come all the way from France, you know? We could have done a mini-auction over Skype."

Elizabeth swotted her hand to deflect her friend's politeness. "It's really no trouble for us. Julian has been meaning to visit his club for months. We miss England if you can believe it."

"Well, I'm so glad you're here. I assume you don't need any introductions. We've got the Astors, the Huntingtons. Over there are the Godrej's: Kumar and his new wife. A few of the Pinfields are here, too — you remember Jane Pinfield, from Stanford?"

"Of course!" Elizabeth looked around excitedly. "There really is everyone in London. And what about Elias? I've heard so many wonderful things."

"Elias," Helena exhaled and grinned with a look of delight. "He really is so… Elias. You'll simply have to meet him. Let's just say for now he's this crazy genius I picked up in Sweden. Certainly a departure from my recent roster. He doesn't produce cosy, furniture art — it's quite striking stuff. Very rooted in ideology. Not everyone's cup of tea, but I'm happy taking the risk. We're exhibiting his Hearts series in Berlin next year. See, that's exactly it: he's Berlin rather than Paris if it makes sense?"

"I know exactly what you mean," Elizabeth nodded. "He's Ingrid's son, right?"

"Yes," Helena cleared her throat. "But it wasn't really like that. I saw his stuff years ago rather by accident, and I knew I had to snap him up. He wasn't easy to persuade, mind. He's a bit of a maverick. Sometimes it's impossible to get hold of him, he barely answers his phone! He goes missing for days at a time on these long walks where he gets his inspiration."

"A real-life tortured soul," Elizabeth bit her lip.

"Exactly."

"Maybe he'll die in a duel of honour after falling in love with a syphilitic prostitute?"

Helena cackled. "Maybe — if anyone would, it'd be Elias!"

"Wouldn't be bad for sales," Elizabeth raised her eyebrows with ironic knowingness.

"You devil," Helena whispered. They glanced around the room.

"So, tell me more about Hearts."

"It's one of Elias's early collections," Helena paused to take a sip of her drink. "It's all about looking inwards to understand each other. We're auctioning half the collection today. There's a good mixture of stuff: something for everyone. I don't want to twist your arm, but I'm expecting the returns to be quite high on this."

"I don't doubt it," said Elizabeth, her face now serious. "I never doubt you. In fact, I've been meaning to tell you: Sylvie Dupont is coming to ours in a few weeks. She's an old friend of Julian's. I wonder if you and Elias would be interested in meeting her?"

Sylvie Dupont, heiress of a French luxury brand conglomerate, was one of the biggest players in the world of art buying. She bought works of art for an exclusive list of private clients and took a share of the appreciated value. She didn't mentor new talent like Helena; she merely furnished the homes of the rich with whatever was to her taste. Her selection was a marker of credibility: she could skyrocket an artist's reputation overnight, adding two noughts to a price tag. With Sylvie as a client, you didn't need anyone else. Helena had longed for an opportunity to do business with her.

"A trip to France could be fun," said Helena. "Elias would love your place." Now, she was thinking about her sculpture. As the centrepiece of the series, it would be the most desirable target for Sylvie. Helena imagined the price she might get for it.

"Great," said Elizabeth. "Then let's fix it up."

"Oh, here he is," Helena glanced around. "Elias! Come and meet Elizabeth."

Lingering on his own in a gap in the room, Elias looked up to notice Helena and her friend. He waved awkwardly and finished his champagne, and then came over.

"Elias, this is Elizabeth," Helena introduced the two of them. "We were childhood besties in Henley. We also crossed paths at Stanford, where I did my master's in business. Did you know I studied in America?"

Elias proffered a limp handshake to Elizabeth. "No, I didn't," he mumbled. "Pleasure to meet you," he said without looking up. There was a short silence.

"We had a great time," Helena continued. "Funnily enough, I don't remember doing much studying."

"Speak for yourself," Elizabeth rolled her eyes. "You were the party animal. I was more of a bookworm, Elias."

"You were," Helena grinned. "She got a first! I think I only managed a 2:2."

"Well, it hardly mattered," said Elizabeth, gazing across the room. "Isn't Helena brilliant? What a fantastic show she puts on."

"Yeah," said Elias, checking over his shoulder.

"I think Elias has turned rather shy," Helena smiled. "Artistic genius is funny — we should probably get ready for the auction. Elias, let's get ready shall we?" The young artist nodded. "Elizabeth, it's been an absolute pleasure. Let's have a drink later and talk about this trip." They kissed each other on the cheek.

"Do try to make a good impression," said Helena as they crossed the room, forcing a cheeriness to various members of the crowd. "Art, unfortunately, doesn't talk, and most people aren't here for it. They're here for *you*, Elias," she turned and smiled at him. To one side of the room, the Hearts collection was being displayed. People crowded around to inspect the various pieces and read the boxes of text before they were put up for auction.

Elias rubbed his face. "I'm not used to this," he said.

"Just follow me," said Helena. "I'll take the lead. Go and grab yourself a drink; try to chill out and don't do anything weird. We're on in five."

"Good evening," Helena gushed over the microphone as the crowd rushed to find their seats. Besides her, at the front of the room, Elias was sitting nervously. "Give it up for Elias Karlsson, my superstar from Malmö. It's a huge honour to auction his work from the iconic Hearts series before it goes on to exhibit in Berlin next year." She beamed at the crowd, glanced at her card and read: "The heart, once considered the vehicle for the soul — the essence of life, the connection between the body and the divine — has seen a cultural demotion to a banal status: a mere pump, replicated by machinery, transplanted casually; a fallible functionary to the organism's continuity. Hearts demands a reconsideration of the contemporary status

61

of this organ. The beating heart — our earliest notion of time passing, the marker of our own time — is afforded new prominence by the artist. In Hearts, Elias Karlsson begs us to love ourselves and one another." The crowd clapped enthusiastically. Elias blushed as Helena turned to join in the applause.

The pieces were presented one at a time. The title, the materials used, and some information about them was read out by Helena. Once everything had been shown, the bidding began. "The Price of Love," Helena announced. "This gorgeous cardioid represents the integrity of love in an era of mass commercialisation. Perhaps it's fitting to start here." She laughed. "Let's start the bidding at a thousand pounds. It's a beautiful piece; I'm jealous of whoever takes it home. Who'll offer me a thousand pounds for the price of love?"

Helena handled the bidding with ease. She knew everyone in the room. She never pushed; she took each price escalation as if it was the final sum, maintaining a look of contentment throughout that detached the event from any transactional motive. "Twenty-five thousand: it's the price of love, after all. Going once, going twice, going to the wonderful Ms. Buckley. What an enviable addition to an already enviable collection. Next up, 'Fuck Off or Finger Me' — this iconic clay figurine will really make a statement in any contemporary collection worth its salt. Let's start this one at five thousand. Good luck to whoever has to get it in the car!" The clay sculpture sold for £62,000 to the girlfriend of an uncle. After that, a series of screen-printed curve functions were snapped up for five figures each.

Odilio was lurking at the back of the room. It was normal for him to feel left out at these things; the art crowd and him didn't naturally gel, but he could normally handle the fake-nice chit-chat and pretentious bores. This evening, Odilio was feeling the full force of rejection. He sensed it in the way people looked at him. He detected suspicion in their furtive glances, something accusative even.

There was a break in the bidding during which half the room charged for the bar. A pair of blue eyes caught Odilio's attention from the stampede and, before he had time to work out who was coming over, Darren Baker, former lacrosse number one at Berkeley and frat-boy extraordinaire, had thrust a meaty hand in his direction, a broad smile unfolding within his podgy head, flashing a grid of wine-stained teeth. "Good to see you, buddy, good to see you," he gripped Odilio's hand.

"Nice to see you, too, Darren," said Odilio.

"What an event. Helena's a star when it comes to this sort of thing. Free bar, too. Let's get wasted!" He gulped down his glass of wine.

Odilio tended to avoid men like Darren Baker. The six-foot-four, two-hundred-and-forty-pound former athlete had shagged his way around half the Berkeley campus, as well as the fringes of many more. He possessed that uniquely oblivious American confidence that only served to bolster his ample self-assurance. Darren Baker's life had peaked during adolescence, and for this, he was a victim of his own making. In his narrowly distorted worldview, he was the main character; everyone else was a functionary, a mere satellite in orbit of the galactic man-child. Odilio, for instance, was the little guy, punching in his marriage, who took eating out too seriously. In this tragic distortion — the hangover of a time when it had better coincided with reality — every woman loved him. Every wife harboured a desire to sleep with him; every man looked up to him with a mixture of insecurity and envy. There was no nuance with Darren, no capacity for self-reflection. He was incapable of seeing other people's value for things he did not already consider himself more valuable in. There was no way of meeting him on any other terms than his own. Odilio knew from experience his best bet with such people was waiting for them to move on.

"Your last column; that really cracked me up," Darren said, adjusting his scrotum through his trousers.

"Thank you," said Odilio, taken aback by the compliment. The interview with Matthew Watts had failed to land as he'd wanted it to. The unfolding allegations against Tony had knocked him back in the days that followed. The piece lacked specificity and, therefore, bite. Cooper had texted Odilio shortly after he'd sent it, saying: *Not bad. Not great*. Odilio had refrained from sharing the online version on Twitter, and so Darren's opinion was only the second piece of feedback he'd received on it.

"I didn't know you read my work," said Odilio.

"Sure I do. Always got a copy of The Gent in my toilet. No offence; I don't read unless I'm taking a shit."

"Of course."

"Yeah, that preachy little veggie you interviewed — what a hateful creep!"

Odilio smiled. "He was a bit hateful."

"A bit!" Darren Baker chuckled. "He was a fucking moron. Fuck him, man. I'd've struggled not to punch his face in." He clenched his hand into a fist. "I can't take that kind of shit from a guy, you know? I can't be talked down to. You have some impressive patience."

"I guess I wouldn't have much of a career if I thumped everyone who pissed me off."

Darren Baker let out a roaring laugh. "Right, let's get some more drinks," he took Odilio's empty glass from his hand. "I must be wasted: I just spent nine thousand on a really ugly painting. Helena says it'll be worth a fortune one day. She better be right!" He roared with laughter again and made his way to the bar.

Odilio scanned the room. The crowd was beginning to coagulate in small groups. Unguarded and open to the thrill of introductions, this was how the wealthy socialised. Elias Karlsson exited the toilet and beelined across the room, straight past Odilio. "Doing great," Odilio called out. The young artist flinched at the remark. "Must be nice earning a bit of money for once!"

Elias glanced at him, and, recognising who he was, came over. "It's not about the money though, is it?" he said, quietly.

Of course it wasn't, thought Odilio. His trust fund probably paid him in a week what Odilio made in a year at The Gent. "You tell me," said Odilio.

"I'm finally being recognised. That's the best part." He rubbed the end of his nostrils together. "Although the money's welcome. I mean, footballers are paid a lot more than us, yet we make *fucking culture*. You hear me?"

"I do," Odilio replied, stifling an urge to burst out laughing. Was the kid on drugs? With a line like that, you had to wonder.

"Still, you have to have some sort of struggle if you want to produce anything real. Wouldn't do us any good driving around in Bugattis." Elias looked around. "Anyway, how are you, man? Helena said you were in a bit of trouble."

"Trouble?" said Odilio.

"That guy you were on TV with... Speared by the whole 'Me Too' thing. Helena told me everything. Said you were pretty cut up by it. Never watched the show, if I'm honest. Bit young for it, plus I don't think it aired in Sweden. Anyway, horrible to learn that about someone you were close to."

Odilio swallowed. Cocky little shit, he thought. Why on earth had Helena told him about Tony? He cleared his throat, feigning a casual expression as he looked around. "Yeah, it's a shame," he said. "Although, he was more of an acquaintance..." Odilio glanced over Elias's shoulder. His wife was being flocked by several of her bidders.

"Guess we have to watch what we do, eh?" said Elias.

"You can never be too careful."

Elias grinned at him before resuming his path across the room.

Odilio approached the crowd that surrounded his wife. She had a gift for dividing her attention between people who wanted all of her own. Odilio recognised one of them as Helena's friend, Michael Lott. The old lech had been in the art world forever. That he leched on men didn't make it any more acceptable, although it seemed to pull the wool over everyone else's eyes — his wife's included. "Extraordinary," Michael crooned into Helena's ear. "He really is something special. What a clever girl you are." He squeezed Helena against him. Odilio looked

66

at them, with their thinning heads of hair, their wet eyes, and felt a shiver of disgust. His wife had always celebrated the art world as a friendlier, less testosterone-fuelled place than the world of fine dining, but Odilio didn't buy it. The art crowd were simply better at hiding themselves. With their camp mannerisms and edgy dress sense, the same creeps lurked in equal measure.

"Ah, Odilio," said Michael, noticing him in the crowd.

"Darling," Helena blew a kiss to her husband.

"Isn't she clever?" Michael said. "I mean, who other than Ms. Courtenay could convince two-hundred witless aristos to part with their money on something as ridiculous as this. We're buying the O-level collection of a teenager! What a laugh you must be having at our expense." His eyes sparkled with humour as he looked around at the braying crowd. "Oh, you must be making a fortune," he burst out laughing. The others laughed, too. "God, he's quite sexy, that Swede. How do you keep your hands off him? Or maybe you don't! Sorry, Odilio!"

"Michael, you're horrid," Helena giggled. "Elias and I are strictly colleagues. I'm old enough to be his mother."

Odilio could muster nothing more than a shit-eating grin in response. He was quite relieved when Darren Baker appeared beside him with two large glasses of red.

11

"Are you annoyed?"

"I'm fine."

"You've been weird all evening."

"I'm just tired."

"What are you thinking about?" Helena asked.

"Nothing," said Odilio, winding down the window so that the cold air could reduce the redness of his cheeks, a consequence of having drunk too much red wine. He was as foggy as he was irritable. Sure, he'd been annoyed before running into Elias — that was the sort of mood you could get over. But bumping into the young artist, enduring his inane pity and self-aggrandizing nonsense — that was what had ruined the night. He was annoyed with Helena for having spoken to Elias about Tony, but mostly he was just annoyed with Elias.

"Well, if you want to be like that, I'm going to ignore you," Helena said, returning her attention to her phone. She was writing to her endless contact list, thanking everyone individually for coming down. The taxi passed Hyde Park in its darkness, down Kensington High Street. Odilio watched the houses pass by in a blur, his thoughts half-formed and bitter. But something was decanting from the murkiness of the past week, something he could hold and use to take action. Planning made him nervous — he'd grown used to the shrouding mental fog and inertia it encouraged — and yet he knew he couldn't persist in such limbo forever.

It was eleven o'clock when they entered the sitting room. Rachel and Stuart were sitting on the sofa. "Hello, everyone," said Odilio, taking off his coat and throwing it across the armchair.

"Good evening my lovelies," Helena gushed, stashing her phone into her clutch bag. "Goodness, it's so late; I can't believe you're still here, Stuart!".

Stuart blushed as he checked the time on his phone. "I've been meaning to go for ages," he chuckled and stood up quickly.

"I told you!" Rachel giggled. "We've been having a lovely natter."

"I'm delighted to hear it," said Helena. "Stuart, you're welcome to stay as long as you like — I hope Maria sorted dinner."

"Everything was great," he said.

"How did the auction go?" asked Rachel, adjusting the blanket over her legs.

"Oh, it was wonderful," said Helena. "Absolutely wonderful. I'm working with a genius. You'll have to meet Elias someday."

"Did you sell much?"

"They couldn't get enough of him," she said with a twinkle in her eye.

Odilio rarely gave much thought to the lives of his staff. Language barriers made it easy to forget that the people who worked for him had internal worlds as complicated as his own. But the presence of these two fresh faces — middle-class, educated, English — reminded him of this oversight. He felt old and misplaced in his sitting room. The feeling was encouraged by a look the au pair gave the tutor: a wide-eyed look he'd never seen in her before. He studied the tutor, with his shabby

69

clothes and messy facial hair, and felt a strange sort of envy. He realised how little he knew about either of them. They came each day, pierced the inner core of his family life, then retreated to wherever, as if watching through one-way glass.

"Rachel, Stuart — let me show you something I think you'll love."

Odilio interrupted: "I think we should let them get going. They've got homes of their own to get back to."

"Don't be silly, darling, it'll take two minutes. Come with me."

They followed Helena upstairs. She whispered as they walked across the landing, so as not to disturb Tabitha who was sleeping on the floor above. They crept into the living room where the sculpture greeted them. Helena ran her hand across the crystal hearts as the others watched on. "So, what do you think, Stuart?"

The tutor's eyes followed up to the naked statue atop the Mr.Whippy-shaped swirl. "Have a good look," said Helena. "I want to know exactly what you're thinking."

"I'm not sure I'm the best person to ask," he said.

"Don't be daft!" Helena laughed. "It's simple: what does it make you feel when you look at it? That's all there is to consider."

"You can say it looks like a giant turd," Odilio snickered.

"Darling, shut up," said Helena. "Stuart, ignore my husband."

The tutor scratched his chin. "I don't feel anything," he said, after some time. "Other than perhaps a desire to work out what it means."

The smile didn't leave Helena's face. "Great," she said. "And that's important in its own way. One mustn't feel they have to like something."

70

The tutor nodded. "I guess I'm a bit old-fashioned in my taste," he said. "I'm more a Water Lilies of Giverny type of guy: the impressionists, that sort of thing."

"I think it's great," said Rachel. She stared at the sculpture with a look of awe. "It's so bold and powerful and — dare I say — feminist?"

"Say it, please," said Helena. "Elias' work is very political." She turned to Stuart. "Well, never mind; my husband doesn't like it either. No shame in that. If you're an impressionist, Stuart, Odilio is the cavalry charge landscapes of the National Gallery." Rachel and Helena both laughed at the remark.

Odilio could feel a headache coming on — a premonition of tomorrow's hangover. Staring at the sculpture only made him feel worse. "On that note, I'm off to bed," he said. "Night, everyone."

"Night night," Helena smiled. "Get a good rest."

"Night, Odilio," said Rachel. He bowed and left the room.

In minutes, he was in his study, trawling through Twitter. The storm surrounding Tony was still raging, although it was entering a new phase of life. The fall of Romano had initiated a ripple effect of accusations against the top names in the restaurant world. Just the other day, the three-Michelin-star Danish chef, Keld Thorsen, was the subject of a lengthy open letter by staff at his Copenhagen flagship, Rune. Thorsen was accused, among other things, of flashing his penis at female staff as well as adding his semen to a cake mix he'd served at a Christmas party. The letter accused the chef of routinely employing sexual humiliation as punishment in his kitchens. Since its publication, Keld Thorsen had gone missing:

71

there were whispers going around the internet that he'd killed himself. Odilio had interviewed Thorsen in Denmark just last year and had described him in that piece as a 'friend', although they'd met, perhaps, on only half a dozen occasions. A conversation was emerging. Questions were being asked — answers were being attempted — how had these men gotten away with it for so long? Why had the culture allowed them to thrive plainly in sight, with no repercussions until it was too late? Odilio had a stack of private messages from various journalists pressing him for his input on the matter. His connections to Tony and, now, Thorsen were too public to ignore. So far, he'd refrained from saying anything. Now was the time to write a statement and put it out there. He would sever ties with Tony, issuing his deepest condolences to the victims, and then he would go offline. He fancied getting out of London.

Odilio paused in front of his open Word document wondering how best to express himself. But something didn't feel right doing it this way. He should meet Tony first and tell him exactly what he was going to do before he did it. Twitter was the coward's way out. He'd write to arrange a meet-up, explaining his thoughts before making them public.

Odilio opened his email. A slew of junk clogged his inbox. Several restaurants invited his custom (this never worked — his assistant assigned each job); restaurants he *had* reviewed wrote back, challenging aspects of his criticism. His accountant had been in touch, recommending he hold onto his Romano & Rome stock; new directorship and a strong PR campaign could turn their value around in a few years. Odilio was scrolling through when he noticed a message that sent a spike of cold shock through him. It was exactly what he was about to write, but now it spun him out being the one to receive it. From Tony Romano.

Odilio clicked it.

Hey, could do with the company of an old friend. What say we meet for a drink? T x

12

"No Stuart today?" Odilio enquired at the doorway of the dining room. At the table, Rachel and Tabitha were cutting up sheets of paper and sticking them to a large piece of card. "Not today," said Rachel, looking over. "It's his day off."

"Stuart never comes on a Wednesday," said Tabitha, her concentration unwavering as Odilio edged to the table to see what they were up to.

"Very nice," he said. "What a wonderful poster."

Rachel nodded. "Not just a pretty face are you Tabs?"

Tabitha said nothing as she coloured in her drawing with felt-tip pens.

"What's it about?" Odilio asked.

"It's history homework," said Rachel. "She's been working on it with Stuart."

"Ah, the discovery of the Americas," said Odilio, registering the textbook on the table. "Very interesting." He tried to recall what he knew on the subject. "Christopher Columbus, 1496? Commonly mistaken as a Spanish citizen: he was neither an Italian national, but, instead, a resident of the Republic of Genoa. Italy, of course, didn't exist back then."

"I didn't know you were such a history buff," Rachel said with an impressed look.

"Well, I read it for O-level. They were tougher qualifications then, too: much harder than the GCSEs nowadays."

"I was an art student," said Rachel, "so I'm useless with this sort of thing. I did get an A in photography, though."

"1492," Odilio muttered to himself, skim-reading the information on the poster. With its colourful spread of text, illustrations, and maps, it was a good-looking piece of work.

"Daddy," said Tabitha, pausing to switch pens. She ensured the lids were on properly by pressing them against the table until they clicked.

"Yes, my darling?"

Tabitha let out a theatrical sigh. "Christopher Columbus didn't discover America, actually. There were already loads of people there when he arrived."

"Sure, sure," said Odilio, shooting Rachel a knowing look. "But Columbus figured out how big the place was — where the whole thing could go on a map. There were some people there, but they were very primitive. They didn't have any maps or ships."

Tabitha pointed to one of the poster's information 'bubbles'. "There were sixty million Americans *before* Columbus arrived and in the next hundred years they were nearly all killed by Columbus and his friends who took them prisoner, spread diseases, and sometimes *ate* them." She shuddered.

Odilio laughed. "I don't think anybody was eaten, sweetheart. And you have to remember lots of his friends were killed by the natives, too. That's history: it's a horrible, gory business…" Noticing what his daughter was colouring in, Odilio trailed off. "Tabitha, you can't write that!"

75

"What?" she looked at him. With a felt-tip pen, she was filling in a bubble-written title that read: 'CHRISTOPHER COLUMBUS: MURDERER'.

"Darling, you can't hand that in."

"Why not?" she said.

"It's... Rachel, what's she meant to be working on?"

"The pros and cons of Columbus's visit to America, I think."

"Christopher Columbus was an evil man," Odilio read aloud from the conclusory bubble. "He killed many people in America and robbed them, too. He was greedy and vicious and even his boss locked him in jail for being too nasty..." Odilio shook his head. "Tabitha, this is very unfair." He pulled a chair next to her and sat down. "This is really forceful; your teacher will think you have an agenda writing stuff like this. Do you know what an agenda is?"

Tabitha shrugged.

"I imagine Stuart encouraged her," Rachel laughed. "He thinks there's an agenda with everything on the curriculum."

"What's an agenda?" asked Tabitha.

"It means you're not being fair," said Odilio. "That you're taking sides. With history, we have to be two-sided. We might not agree with everything Columbus did, but it's important we see things from his perspective, too. Those were different times. We can't give every historical figure a kicking just because we don't agree with them today." He tapped on the poster with his fingers. "I think we can do better than this, Tabs. When's it in for?"

"Tomorrow," she said.

"Rachel, please can you stay until she's finished?"

"Sure," Rachel replied. "Although I'm not an expert on any of it!"

"Just make it balanced. I don't want the school to think her parents are cranks." Odilio forced a grin as he pinched Tabitha on the ear. He stood up. "It's pros and cons, remember. So try and get some more of the positives in there. Rachel, find an essay online."

13

"I'm drifting from Tabitha," said Odilio, climbing into bed. Helena was messing about on her iPad with an app that could adorn a photographic rendering of a house in different wallpaper styles.

"What do you mean?" she said, her eyes fixed to the screen.

Odilio shimmied under the duvet. "I hardly see her," he said. "She always has someone around. If it isn't Rachel, it's the tutor: if it isn't him, it's someone else. She's busier than anyone I know." Helena reached out a hand and rubbed his chest. "I feel like we don't spend enough time together. The house is too big. It's so big we can be in at the same time and completely miss each other."

"We're just busy," said Helena. "You're forgetting what a good thing that is. Imagine being crammed together here all day. You'd go mad in a week, you know that, darling." She clicked a button on her iPad that changed the skin of the rendering. "Of course, if you'd like, we could cut some of Rachel's hours. Tabs has Stuart four evenings a week; Rachel's just sitting around waiting for bedtime. We could keep her on for the school run but send her home as soon as he arrives?"

"And *we* do bedtime?" said Odilio.

"Mhmm."

"We can't every night," he shook his head. "I can't fight to get Tabitha in the bath, and I don't have time to read her a bedtime story."

"We could alternate it, work in shifts?"

"I'd have to think about it."

"You could try tutoring her," Helena laughed.

Odilio studied the look on his wife's face. "I'd be good at it," he said, seriously.

"I'm sure you would."

"It might be good for her to have some balance."

"How so?" Helena rested the iPad against her knees.

"I've been thinking," said Odilio. "He's very opinionated, this Stuart chap."

"You only ever say that about someone you disagree with."

Odilio twisted onto his side. "Actually, I disagree with him on lots of things."

"I don't believe it," Helena smiled.

Odilio reached forward and took his wife's hand. He stroked the back of her wrist with his fingers. "Tabs is only nine. Children that age — girls especially — are very susceptible to what other people think."

"Aren't we all?" said Helena.

"I think his views are a little out there. I don't think it's good for Tabitha, particularly at that age, to be exposed to them all."

"Such as?"

"It's hard to give an example." He shuffled so that he was sitting level with his wife. "I mean, it sounds silly, but even the fact that he's a vegetarian... He's telling Tabitha it's wrong to eat meat. Sure, it's his opinion, but it's not ours. We do

79

eat meat. *She* eats meat. If he's telling her one thing and we're doing another, then I don't know how good it is for her view on us."

Helena frowned. "Tabby's smarter than that. She doesn't absorb every opinion like a bloody sponge. Stuart is interesting to her, undoubtedly. She hasn't met anyone like him before. But he's completely harmless, like a court jester. Sure, he's different from us — it's natural he intrigues her. But she still sees the world like we do, I know that." She freed her hand from Odilio's and went back to clicking her iPad.

"I've had an idea," said Odilio. "Why don't we go on holiday, the three of us? It's half-term soon, isn't it?"

"It's next week," said Helena.

"Let's go to Scotland. We can stay at your brother's place, get out in the fresh air and spend some quality time together."

Helena thought for a moment. "It's not a bad idea," she said.

"It's a great idea," said Odilio. "I could share what I know with Tabs — all the stuff Dad taught me. A bit of bonding time together. It would be nice to see Phillip, too."

"It's been a while since we last went to Aviemore," Helena pondered.

Odilio was suddenly animated. He was thinking of the Trossachs. Long days out with his father, learning to fish, shoot, and hunt red stags. They were some of the most thrilling experiences of his life. Deep down, Odilio had always wanted a son to share these experiences with. Helena had been content with their little girl. A second child was off the cards; Helena hated everything about her pregnancy, from its two-pronged assault on her career and figure to the dependency it created on others. Never again. Adoption was floated as a concession, but Odilio had put his foot down there. In adoption, he saw a reckless gamble with genetics — the potential for nasty surprises only to be revealed when it was too late. The matter had quietly settled itself, although he wondered, perhaps more than his wife, what others thought about their slimline family arrangement.

"I could take her hunting; we could shoot red stags. That'll get any silly vegetarian ideas out of her head!" Odilio sat up in bed.

Helena frowned. "She's too young to use a rifle."

"Well, she could see it done. I'd take her fishing, too. We could go on walks, teach her how to cook together. It would be nice to get out of London."

"I'd need to speak to Phillip first," said Helena. "You know how he runs the estate. It's rare for them not to have guests, especially at such late notice."

Years ago, when Odilio's brother-in-law was still drinking, he'd hosted lavish hunting weekends at the estate, during which a braying pack of old boys came together to drink, smoke, and shoot in roughly that order. Odilio recalled those weekends with a fondness buffered only by Phillips' U-turn to sobriety. The new Phillip was structured and orderly. These days, they saw each other significantly less.

"I wonder if he still has the same gamekeeper?" said Odilio. "Father Tom: what a character. Some of us owe our lives to that man." Father Tom was almost a parody of highland propriety: the gamekeeper by day, he became the party's babysitter at night when things threatened to spill over, and someone had to take

81

charge. On more than one occasion, Father Tom had been forced to confiscate the weaponry of a particularly inebriated hunting party.

"No idea," said Helena. "I'll give him a ring this week and find out. It's a good plan."

"It's perfect," said Odilio, easing into the pillow. Aviemore in the Cairngorms: the thought of its misty mornings filled him with the sort of comfort he hadn't experienced in a long time. He couldn't wait to get out of London.

14

"So, I've scrapped the film idea. It'll be a written piece of work, focusing on the actions of Elias Karlsson, and the inferences drawn about me by a team of spies, who follow me around for twenty-four hours a day." Elias paused to sip his drink. It was his fourth in the hour and he was talking quickly. The bar of the Shoreditch hotel in which they were sitting had an unbelievably high ceiling. Like the nave of a cathedral, it reverberated with the conversations of the tables around them, such that one had to talk louder and faster if they wanted to get a word in. Helena was listening with a pained expression. She sunk into the tacky piece of pink furniture. Elias responded by leaning forward, barking the contents of his mind as if encouraged by her retreat.

"The piece will include every strand of their observations amalgamated on a single scroll," he continued. "It's going to be one hundred metres long, rolled out across the exhibition floor. Members of the public can sit, stand or lie on it, and read the scroll at their leisure. The conclusions of the spies will be such that the astute viewer," he paused to rub his nose, which made a strange, squelching noise as he did, "will be able to infer the discords and accords that exist between the observers and observed through the incompleteness of the inferences made by the former. Those who know me will appreciate the shortcomings of the account, which will be bolstered by the publication of a mixed-media journal I keep over the same period.

It's a criticism of the third-person perspective and, therefore, of all art since the beginning of time."

Helena had been around long enough to know what was going on. She didn't have many opinions — not of the moral sort, at least — when it came to using powders. But she did know they were bad for business. Cocaine's marketers had pulled off a devilish trick convincing people there was a high-functioning aspect to their product. In reality, standards dropped embarrassingly low on it, while a Christ-like sense of grandeur took hold. Helena had quickly lost track of what the young artist was telling her.

Elias had gone too far with that last line, and now he was on edge as a numbing sensation worked its way through his gums that told him he was high. Sober, he was shy to the point of concern, but if coke helped him regain his confidence, what was the harm in a little bit of it? Unfortunately, on this occasion, he'd missed the sweet spot. Helena only wanted to discuss money, but Elias couldn't care less. Here was a fresh idea, cutting edge, and she wasn't having any of it. He stared across the table. In the dusky-pink light of the room, she was too gorgeous to stay annoyed at. Like all beautiful people, Elias would find a way to forgive her.

Helena tried to steer the conversation back on topic. "Look," she said. "We really need to talk about this exhibition in Berlin—"

"I know, I know," Elias interrupted. "And I reckon we should still do that."

"We have to do that," said Helena, firmly. "We're basically contracted to."

"Sure, sure, and we will do that." Elias licked his lips.

"We made six figures at the auction. Now we need to make your work sing in an exhibition."

"It'll sing alright," Elias smiled before necking the rest of his drink. He gestured towards the bar for another. "All I'm saying is — imagine for a second what I'm saying is — *fuck it.* Fuck them, okay? You bought our art, now stomach it. We don't stick to a plan. Elias Karlsson does what he wants, and if he wants to go to Hong Kong and make a piece on Chinese state surveillance, then so be it. Why take Hearts to Berlin now? It's boring. I did it years ago. I can't even remember what it's about. Instead, we drop a totally new piece on them, a totally different conceptual angle, country, theme, etcetera. It keeps me fresh; it keeps them guessing. They buy more."

"Listen," Helena snapped. Elias withdrew in his chair, satisfied with the reaction he'd provoked in her. When he wound her up enough that a crack formed in her composure, a ray of light shone through that offered him hope. It was hope that she didn't just see him as Ingrid's son: a young idiot she was doing a favour for. It was hope that things weren't all well with her husband and that something soon might happen between them. Yes, he had hope when he annoyed her because it was proof she regarded him with more importance than the innumerable things she navigated daily with ease, for which her composure never seemed to let up.

Helena tucked her hair behind her ears and sipped her wine. "If we don't do that exhibition, if we don't back that auction up as best as we can, then my name — and certainly yours — will be mud. You've had one successful auction, but that doesn't mean you can do what you want yet. To put it politely: people don't give a shit about you. Bail on it all now, and you'll be blacklisted as someone investors want nothing to do with. Do you think you can go it alone? This is not the Belle Epoque — it's serious business. At the moment, you're someone to take seriously. Why? Because I told people to take you seriously. I also told them you'd make them serious money. So that's what you and I are going to do. Then, ten years down the line, when you're exhibiting in the Tate: when you've headlined the Sotheby's auction list, you can go to Hong Kong and do whatever it is you need to do about Chinese CCTV. But it's too early to play rock star, okay? You can do that later when we're done."

The waiter arrived with Elias' drink. "Another sazerac cocktail," they said. "Will that be all?"

"Just the bill when you're ready, please," Helena said.

"I'm going for a cigarette," said Elias.

"Sit down," said Helena, who was on a roll. "I've been chatting with my friend, Elizabeth. You met her briefly at the auction. A lovely woman — she lives in a beautiful spot on the French Riviera with her husband. Anyway, she's friends with a very exciting mover in the art world. Sylvie Dupont. She's visiting their place next weekend and Elizabeth has asked us over. If we're lucky, it could be an in. Sylvie will look after us if we can get her on board. Are you interested?"

Elias shrugged. "It's something I'd be interested in," he said absently. Of course, he was interested. A trip to the South of France with Helena, raking it in together off some old bint with more money than sense. What was there not to like?

"Good," said Helena. "Then I'll let her know we're coming." She took her phone from her bag and started texting.

Elias stood up. "I'm going for that cigarette," he said.

15

The rain-soaked pavements glistened beneath the street lamps as the taxi sped through the evening traffic. Odilio was on his way to The Groucho. It was his first time meeting Tony in over a year, and he was trying to pinpoint exactly when that last was. Tony, for his many vices, had always made the effort with their friendship. There were the food hampers at Christmas, the birthday money for Tabitha; the anniversary gifts. It was Tony who organised their annual get-togethers, even when he lived on the other side of the world. Odilio wouldn't have bothered otherwise. A night out with Tony Romano was an exercise in binge drinking, stamina, and turning a blind eye to his worst excesses. In recent years, Odilio had vowed never again. So it was true they were drifting long before his proclivities were exposed for the world to see. Severing ties with his old friend had been a long time coming; Odilio couldn't be accused of doing anything snakeish. Tonight, he would draw a line under twenty-five years of friendship. It was time to move on. He imagined Tony would have some grand plan — he'd talked before about setting up a seafood shack in Cuba. Well, now was his chance. Go to Cuba, old friend. Go and start again, away from London, away from your disgrace....

Of course, Odilio would never forget all the help he'd received over the years. They'd met when Odilio was a trainee reporter, when he, too, had a taste for long debauched nights, drugs, women, and Michelin-star food. The stars had aligned. Tony had introduced the young Odilio to some of the top names in the industry, letting them know that this plucky young restaurant critic was an approved man — someone the industry could trust in. It made Odilio a tempting option to promote, seeing him lauded for his ability to gel with the other side of the restaurant floor. As Odilio climbed the greasy pole, Tony helped him sort table after table at the most exclusive restaurants. Later, it was Tony who invited Odilio to work on the show, having rejected every candidate the producers put forward.

But Tony was surely finished, now. There was no coming back from this, no future in their friendship. He would meet Tony for a drink. One drink. He would let him know he was disgusted to hear of the allegations against him. He would mention the statement he planned to release: that he was coming out in defence of the numerous women who'd accused Tony of the most shameful behaviour. There would be no ties between them after tonight. It was time to jump ship before it torpedoed into the ocean floor.

Tony was sitting on his own at the back of the club. The Groucho wasn't an ideal location to keep a low profile, but it was their usual spot, and Tony had insisted. He leapt from his chair when he noticed Odilio enter. "You're a good boy," he said, grasping him in his arms. Odilio stood limply in Tony's embrace. They sat down, the waiter arrived, and Odilio ordered an Old Fashioned. "Make that two," said Tony.

"It's always been so neat in here," Odilio said, filling in the silence. "You can't go wrong with classical interiors."

"A bit louche for me," said Tony. He fiddled with his napkin, folding the corners with a purposefulness that looked like he was making origami, then gave up

89

and threw the napkin onto the table, shaking his head as tears built up in his eyes. "It's been the hardest week of my life," he sobbed before burying his head into his hands.

Tony Romano had never been a good looking man. Of his personality, the most generous thing you could say was that he was 'larger than life': a back-slapping joker with a roaring, chain-smoker's laugh. That unique laughter — like the sound of an angle grinder — filled any room he was in. In less boisterous moments, he was easy on the eye, and in a serious mood (and in a good suit) he looked like an extra from *Goodfellas*. A half-Sicilian raised in Birmingham, he played up to the Mediterranean side of his heritage enthusiastically. With shiny hair, Brylcreemed to his head; his stocky physique gave him the quality of a mafia bruiser. His penchant for the eccentric; his 'I don't give a fuck' outfits: pastel suits on his days off, and, at work, faded tracksuit bottoms, chef's crocs, and novelty socks. In the London scene, Tony was as good as the real deal. Those were the good things you could say about him. But this was not Tony on a good day. Looking into those tired, red eyes, new bags forming under the old ones, Odilio thought he could see death.

The waiter arrived with their drinks. Tony's face changed as they were placed on the table. "And two more in two minutes," he said, reaching for his Old Fashioned. "Cheers!" They clinked glasses. Tony finished his in one go, then smacked his lips together, easing back into the chair. Odilio glanced around. The club room was quiet. He checked the neighbouring tables to see if there was anyone he knew.

"It's been a week from hell," said Tony. Grey stubble smattered the jowls of his usually well-groomed face. A rash had formed around his neck where his skin chafed his shirt collar. "A week from fucking hell, I'm telling you."

"I can only imagine."

"I was set up," Tony eyed him. "They tricked me." He lowered his gaze to the table. "It's a mess, a complete fucking mess. But what can you do?" Odilio sipped his Old Fashioned, thinking that there was too much orange zest in the drink. He would let Tony continue talking; he would not give him the affirmation he was looking for.

"They'd been chatting like that the whole shift," said Tony, hesitantly, as if recounting an eyewitness testimony before court. "I was uncomfortable, myself; I just wanted to fit in. They were young lads — you know what they can be like. Mouthy little shits with one thing on their mind. I was just giving it back a little. Well, the second something comes out of *my* mouth, it gets filmed. They uploaded it on the internet for Christ's sake."

"That's terrible, Tony," Odilio winced.

"Too right, but what can you do? I'm at a loss, mate."

"I was talking about you the other week," said Odilio, changing the subject. Tony's intensity was putting him off. He needed small talk before they could get down to business. "I was reading through some of my old columns. Remember the opening night of Seppa?"

"How could I forget?" said Tony, unenthusiastically.

"What a night." Odilio shook his head. Tony studied him, curious as to where he was going. "I wrote a rave review," Odilio added.

"Which you owed me," Tony sniffed. "Your address book must have doubled that evening. I put you in contact with the BBC's head of food."

"You did," nodded Odilio. "Who I went on to work for. But Seppa deserved the praise it got. The food was outstanding. I still think about that roast partridge from time to time."

Tony grunted. "The staff have taken a vote of no confidence in me. Seppa's no longer mine. Good fucking riddance, I hope the ceiling collapses."

At that moment, the waiter arrived with another pair of Old Fashioneds. His presence at the table encouraged Odilio to finish the first one. "Can you bring the bourbon menu when you have a minute?" Tony asked.

"Sure," the waiter bowed out.

"I'm not having... a late one," said Odilio, who had conceded a few drinks might make it easier to be straightforward.

"They've got a new scotch buyer," said Tony, matter-of-factly. "I want to see the spread." He sipped the second drink, clicked his tongue and sat back in his chair. "Too much zest," he said.

"Exactly what I was thinking," said Odilio, who could feel himself softening off the alcohol. "So, how are you coping?" he added after a long pause.

"I'm alright," said Tony. "Not much to do when you're out of work other than get steamed every night." He nodded to his drink. "Now, I understand the losers who blow their dole on White Ace. What else can you do when none of the days have any purpose?"

The waiter returned with the bourbon menu. Tony skimmed through it as the waiter lingered by his side. "Two of these when you're ready," he pointed to the page.

"Excellent choice, sir," said the waiter, collecting the menu.

"Anyway, what have I got to live for now?" said Tony, reaching for the cherry in his glass and popping it into his mouth. "Might as well piss my money away until they find me face down in a hot tub full of sick." He rested his forehead on his arm and started crying again.

Odilio wanted to say something encouraging. He didn't know what to say. "It'll all blow over in a few years." The words seemed to burst from his mouth.

"I haven't got a few years," Tony snapped, his eyes full of tears. "I've worked every day since I was fifteen. This'll be the death of me, mark my words. Inactivity always is, plus, my business is going down the pan. Financially, I'm fucked. No, I can't let those rats get away with it. I need this sorted."

"But what can you do?" Odilio glanced at him. "The video will stick against your word."

"There's not much I can do," he said. He let the silence linger. "But you could help me. There's a favour you might be able to do for me. No pressure, of course, but it would be very helpful."

"Go on," said Odilio.

"I need a spokesperson. Someone who isn't afraid to stick their head above the parapet and say: 'Tony isn't like that. He's been unfairly treated here'. Someone who could vouch for the fact those pricks set me up. Someone who knows I'd never talk like that for no reason. You've worked with me, haven't you?"

"I have," Odilio nodded.

"There you go. So you know what a load of horse shit this is."

Odilio bit his tongue. He took a sip of his drink. "But what about the others?" he said.

"What do you mean?"

"Dozens of others are accusing you of the same thing."

"Nothing substantiated," said Tony, casually. "One video and a heap of lies. Everyone uses my name if it'll get them five minutes of attention. That's why I need friends like you to have my back." He scratched the newly-formed stubble on his cheeks. Flecks of beard dandruff fell to the table. "People would believe you over them," he looked at Odilio, who was thinking back to their years in television together. The show's crew had a nickname for Tony: Ginger Vishnu. He seemed to have multiple pairs of hands that could find themselves anywhere at any time. Shooting in Tyneside one episode, Tony had got blind drunk in the Premier Inn they were staying and had paid for prostitutes with the producer's credit card. The transaction reference 'Steakhouse' saved someone their job; the £800 was written off as an expense in place of a staff Christmas dinner. So it went working with Tony: he took a shit, everyone else cleaned it up.

94

The waiter arrived with the whiskeys. Each contained a double measure of scotch and a single, solid ice cube. The waiter placed them on the table. Tony swirled the tumbler and sniffed the vapours of the double-casked malt. "You know, I had a lot of friends in this city. Lots of people used me when it was convenient for them. Yet here I am, on my own, up shit creek without a paddle, and no one's saying a word. All these 'friends' have suddenly gone silent." Odilio nodded concessively. He wanted to delve into those testimonies against Tony: to get into the meat of the accounts that attested to the most shameful behaviour. It suddenly dawned on him that his friend wasn't interested in redemption — surely impossible, now — but rather in sharing the sabotage; Tony wanted to take others down with him.

"I'm not accusing you of anything, by the way," said Tony. "It's not a threat: I'm simply pointing out that you have a platform. One that could make a real difference in my struggle. Surely it wouldn't cost you much to put a good word out in my defence. Anyway, it's just a suggestion." He held up his whiskey glass. "Cin-cin." He smiled, waiting for Odilio to pick up his own.

At that point, Odilio might have said: "Listen Tony, I don't believe you. I've known you for years: you have a dangerous detachment from reality and an extraordinary ability to see yourself as a victim. The truth is quite the opposite. I believe every woman who has shared their experience at your hands. I believe them not only because of their plurality, their consistency, and the simple fact there is rarely anything to gain in false accusations, but also because I've seen you behave, on numerous occasions, in a way that undermines acceptable standards of behaviour. I've stayed quiet in the past; you seem to have a hold on me that stems back to when I met you. Well, not anymore, you don't. I will do everything to help those women in their bid to destroy you. I will testify in any court in any country as to the person I know you are and the things I have seen you do. Truthfully, I hope there's nothing left of you when they're done. As for you and I: we're finished. As of this moment, there is no you and I."

He might have said this and more, before standing to go, but, instead, Odilio said nothing. Rather than refusing the drink, he took it. "Cin-cin," he mumbled. Tony's proposal had neutralised one he was about to proffer. He could say nothing more than: "Listen, Tony. I really don't want to get involved."

"Have a think about it," Tony watched him.

"I need to."

"You've got time." Tony reached a hand across the table, resting it on Odilio's own.

"It's complicated."

"No one knows that better than me." His gaze had a familiar intensity that caused Odilio to turn away. The moment wasn't right, he thought.

"Let's have another drink."

So other drinks followed, the moment was never right, and soon the moment was lost. The night dissolved into a blur of half-formed excuses and justifications; half-meant concessions and assents; self-pitying speeches that wore Odilio down until he agreed with everything Tony was saying. Soon they were drunk enough to let it go: to begin boorish musings on the value of friendship; the usual anecdotes exchanged. More drinks — relapses into self-pity — then cogency was all but lost. Tony Romano stumbled into a reserve of gin-soaked happiness. Song-singing and table-drumming ensued. They bid farewell on the doorstep of The Groucho under conditions Odilio wouldn't fully remember other than a lingering sense he'd promised something he couldn't deliver. Lying in bed that night, Odilio hoped Tony would forget those promises, too.

16

"I chatted to Phillip, everything is going ahead," Helena called from the en suite. "We can stay the whole week. Isn't that lovely of him? He'll be there, too, of course."

"That's great news," said Odilio, who was lying on the bed, staring out the window. It wasn't even five o'clock, and already it was dark outside. When the days shortened, Odilio felt an intense urge to hibernate. This evening, the urge was compounded by the viciousness of his hangover. No amount of water seemed able to hydrate his mouth, which was sticky with thick saliva. Paracetamol hadn't curbed the pulsating sensation in his head. It was his worst hangover in years, perhaps since his early twenties. Odilio lowered himself into bed, imagining the 15-tog, goose-down duvet was a nest in which he could sleep through winter.

Helena appeared at the doorway of the bathroom. She was halfway through applying a face mask. "Laurene won't be about, though. She had to go to Panama at the last minute — urgent accounting issues, apparently. I think Phillip is quite pleased to have us. I imagine he gets lonely there without her." She dipped back into the bathroom. Through the window, Odilio watched as the silhouette of a tree branch, illuminated by a street lamp, jerked manically in the wind.

"That's a shame," he said, automatically. Phillip's wife was hardly motivation for the trip. Indeed, Phillip tended to be sharper on his own. Helena had come to a similar assessment before.

"Aren't you excited, darling?"

"Very," he groaned. Just moving his head reminded him of how much it hurt.

"It was your idea, after all."

"And it's a great idea," he called back. Any respite from the way he was feeling seemed like a great idea at this point. He thought of the clean highland air, the dewy pastures, void of human life, and grew a new depth to his longing to be there.

"Good, because I'm going to need you there all week," Helena said.

"And where will you be?" he asked.

"I'll join you all later. I'm visiting the Walkers' place in Antibes with Elias."

"Right," said Odilio, vacantly. The last time Helena visited their renovated estate on the Riviera, she'd returned with a lingering need to relay its awfulness in detail. The Walkers' converted chateau was tacky, brash, and screamed of new money, according to Helena, who vowed never to return again.

"It's not a holiday," said Helena, as if reading his mind. "Sylvie Dupont will be there. She's a friend of Julian's. Elizabeth invited us. It would be amazing to build a relationship with her."

"I imagine it would," said Odilio, rubbing his temples. His wife's childhood friend had come into a fortune marrying the patent-holder of the world's most legally harmful plastic explosive. The idea that Sylvie Dupont was a friend of

Julian's amused Odilio greatly. Such was the confusedness of establishment networks.

"You're hungover, aren't you darling?" Helena returned to the bedroom.

"Extremely," he smiled back. It was a rare, somewhat nostalgic experience to spend the day so uselessly loitering around the house. He drank regularly but knew his limits, aware of the invisible line, which when crossed, disturbed his sleep and left him irritable and sensitive the next day. The night before had dragged him deep into this miserable territory. Today, he was paying the price. Not that it was his fault, he considered. The arrangement was, in hindsight, doomed to this inevitability. The drinks hadn't stopped flowing, each one coinciding with the promise of some imminent epiphany on his friend's part as if feinting the self-reflections to get Odilio to stay for one more. For Tony Romano, 'no' was an invitation to challenge the taboos of excess.

"Who were you out with? I didn't hear you get in."

"I saw Tony," Odilio said. Just mentioning the name brought back unpleasant memories; realisations Odilio would have liked to ignore.

"You saw him?"

"At The Groucho. He insisted."

"Did he?" Her body language implored him to say more. Odilio could feel his stomach churn. He'd failed in the simple task of cutting ties with Tony. Failed so badly he'd given the impression he was on his side — perhaps even had said so much in words. He remembered the end of the night only in fragments. The shame of his failure persisted in place of any recollection of their conversation. The

100

association was almost synaesthetic: in recalling an image of Tony sitting opposite him, Odilio had a feeling of guilt he hadn't experienced since his Presbyterian primary school.

"I gave him a piece of my mind," said Odilio. "Told him he's a disgrace and that I've no sympathy for him." He studied his wife's face for her reaction.

"But you ended up getting sozzled together?"

Odilio nodded concessively. "We had a lot of ground to cover after that. I mean, he knows he's done wrong. Of course, I told him I won't stand by him — he's on his own for whatever he wants to do next. But we had twenty-five years to wrap up. It wouldn't have felt right leaving straight away. Last night was a send-off of sorts."

Helena watched him, her expression neutral. She smiled and rubbed his legs through the duvet. "Well done, darling, you did the right thing. I'm proud." She stood up. Helena had always been generous in not probing an explanation too hard. Maybe she simply trusted him. Perhaps she believed the truth came out in other, more reliable ways. Helena returned to the bathroom. Odilio's relief that his lie had worked quickly subsided into further disappointment.

The phone rang on the bedside table. It was Phillip. Odilio hesitated before answering. "Phillip, how are you?" There was a fit of coughing down the line, then the familiar, plummy accent of his brother-in-law.

"Odilio! A little birdie tells me you're coming to the Glendales next week."

101

"That's right," said Odilio, sitting up in bed. There was something soothing hearing Phillip's voice, which was almost cartoonish in its warbling poshness. Phillip was only a few years older than Odilio, but his accent seemed to belong to a different century.

"Well, that's just fantastic," said Phillip. "I hear there's a bit of a mission with your visit, too. Get that urbanite Tabitha out of her shell and give her a good dose of highland medicine!"

"Exactly," Odilio laughed. "She's been showing vegetarian tendencies recently."

"We can't have that. I think a course in angling will be a good start, and then we'll have to nab a stag while you're here. It's the season, after all. Might try to shoot a few of the hares that seem to think the Glendales is their personal play area...."

"Sounds great, Phillip," said Odilio, excitedly. The images forming in his mind allayed the wretched anxiety loop he'd been replaying all day. A family holiday was exactly what he needed to put the last few weeks to rest.

"See you on Saturday," said Phillip.

"Can't wait," said Odilio, hanging up the phone.

*

He was downstairs before seven. His hangover was beginning to lift, helped, in part, by a large gin and tonic. In the dining room, Tabitha was finishing her tutorial with Stuart.

"How's she getting on?" Odilio asked, appearing in the doorway. "Still giving poor old Columbus a kicking?" he chuckled, peering at the work on the table.

"Not today, I'm afraid," said Stuart, tapping the textbook with his pencil. "Science," he added.

"Science," echoed Tabitha, who was too focused on her work to look up.

Odilio skirted the dining table.

"We're looking at climate change and the things people can do to prevent the world from getting warmer," said Stuart.

"Cycle to school instead of taking the car," Odilio read aloud. "Recycle used cans and bottles. All pretty straightforward stuff."

"Exactly," said the tutor. "We're discussing more radical options, too. Maybe you can explain those, Tabitha?"

Tabitha looked up. "Never go on an aeroplane," she said. "And don't eat beef."

Odilio chuckled again. The tutor also laughed. "We've been looking at how the cattle industry is one of the biggest contributors to climate change. Flying a dozen times a year doesn't help, either. Anything else, Tabitha?"

"Concenrete."

"Concrete," corrected Stuart. "What's bad about that?"

"Because concrete makes acid rain which is bad for rivers."

"Spot on," said Stuart. "Well done."

Odilio took a seat at the table. The amused smirk didn't leave his face, as he leafed through the pages of the textbook. "It's tricky, isn't it?" he said, scanning a page. "Getting the balance right. Everything is so political nowadays."

"How so?" the tutor replied.

"I mean the curriculum," said Odilio. "Having a balanced curriculum."

"Balance is sometimes a problem, actually," the tutor adjusted his position in the chair.

"Oh, really?"

"Too often issues are presented as having more sides than there are. Climate change, for instance. It's happening. There's not much more to say about it other than trying to sort it out."

"Interesting," said Odilio. "And you'd say the same about Columbus?"

The tutor thought for a moment. "With Columbus it's the opposite problem, actually. There are two sides, but we only ever hear one. Actually, there are hundreds of perspectives that are rarely considered. The views of his contemporaries, those of the natives he captured and tortured. They should be as part of the curriculum as anything. We miss the truth when we reduce an entire era of colonisation down to the word 'discovery'."

Odilio sensed Tabitha was listening carefully to the tutor's speech. He cleared his throat. "When I was your age, Stuart, I had very strong beliefs. I used to think I knew everything. But as you get older, you soften up a bit. We become gentler with age because we gain perspective. We realise how little we know —

how little we knew when we were young — and how small a life is such that it's impossible to understand everything in one go."

The tutor nodded politely.

"Daddy," said Tabitha. "I need to get on with my homework."

"One second, Tabitha." He glanced at Stuart. "We become more forgiving as we get older. The world works in mysterious ways, and works it does, because it's kept going and has done for years. Sometimes our big ideas aren't as good as we think they are. Sometimes we have to remind ourselves to respect the world a bit more and not spend so much time criticising it. Would you say that was fair?"

"I think so," said Stuart.

"Anyway, I didn't mean to distract you," Odilio said, who had considered going on, but was satisfied to have had the last word. "I've actually got a little surprise for Tabitha. Would she like to hear it?"

"Yes please!" Tabitha turned at once.

"Are you ready? This half-term your uncle Phillip has invited us to his huge house in Scotland. We're going up next week."

"Yay!" said Tabitha — a hint of disappointment that the surprise wasn't a new toy.

"We're going to have a big adventure, all of us. We'll go hunting, fishing, and mountain climbing. We'll cook meals on the open fire. We'll have to find the food first, of course."

"That sounds fantastic, doesn't it, Tabitha?" said Stuart.

Tabitha nodded at both of them.

"You're going to learn how to use a rifle. We'll drive jeeps through the mud. I'm going to teach you everything your grandfather taught me."

"Can we ride ponies?" Tabitha asked.

Odilio laughed. "I'm sure we can," he said, ruffling her hair. "Phillip has everything up there. Oh, it's such a wonderful place," he turned to the tutor. "Magic, really. Aviemore: the other side of the Cairngorms. Mountains as far as the eye can see. All kinds of fascinating wildlife. You wouldn't believe you were in Britain."

"I know it well," said the tutor. "I hiked the area with some friends a few years ago. A magical place, indeed."

"Mhmm," said Odilio. "I mean, this estate… It's Helena's brother's and it's enormous. He picked it up for a bargain, with more rooms than you'd know what to do with, in fact—" the enthusiasm rose in his voice. "Would you like to come for the week? Tabitha would love that, wouldn't you, Tabs? There are hundreds of rooms; you'd have your own corner of the house. Rachel's joining, I imagine. You could do some tutorials in the morning, then you'd have the rest of the day to do with as you pleased."

"It's very generous," said Stuart, checking his phone calendar. "I'd need to look at the dates first. I might have to move some stuff around. It's next week, right?"

"It is," said Odilio. "Well, it's entirely up to you."

Odilio wondered if the tutor would get on with Phillip. Helena's brother embodied every vice and virtue of the country gentleman, with his love of highland tradition and all the eccentricities permissible in rural life. A stickler for details, when they'd purchased the estate, originally as a holiday home, Phillip had thrown himself into learning the ways of highland life with boyish enthusiasm. He hadn't scrimped a penny surrounding himself with the best educators in the field. Of course, he had plenty of free time: Phillip had leaned comfortably into the life of the idling aristocrat. Within a few years, the estate had become his full-time residence. These days, he scarcely returned to London. In just as long, his personality had shifted into something nearing clerical. The old, troubled Phillip had found calm in nature. He'd achieved that elusive thing for most people — recovering addicts in particular — which was a genuine connection to the landscape around him.

Odilio's trips to the house were exercises in the grittier of Scottish traditions. When he'd shot his first red stag on Phillip's land, it had been necessary to douse his face in the still-warm blood of the animal. They had snared grouse and plucked them alive, doing their best to avoid the manic pecking of the pain-addled creature: a tradition that was said to improve the quality of the meat as well as to ease the procurement of feathers. It would be amusing to observe the tutor in such an environment. Perhaps it would be a lesson for the young lad. Out in the glens on a freezing morning, when it's you and your prey, nothing else matters. The ancient sense of kill or be killed. New aspects of the spirit came sharply into focus.

"Can I let you know this weekend?" said Stuart.

"We're heading up on Friday," said Odilio. "But I guess you could join afterwards."

"Great," he said. "Then it shouldn't be a problem."

"I'll let you get on." Odilio stood up. "Tabitha, what should I tell Maria to make for dinner?"

Tabitha looked up from her worksheet. "Pizza," she grinned.

"Pizza for the lady," Odilio called out, closing the dining room door as he left.

17

The taxi dropped them off at Euston station. Odilio stepped out of the car. The typical commotion of a Friday night in the city was starting around them. Tabitha and Rachel followed through the packed station building, wheeling their luggage cases as Odilio searched for the tickets on his phone. Tabitha was filled with nervous excitement walking beside her father. She'd never ridden in a sleeper train before and imagined a cosy, four-poster bed in a wood-panelled bedroom, rocking gently as the train hurtled through the night. She anticipated hot cocoa from the snack cart and views of rolling, moonlit fields as her father told riveting ghost stories about children on trains from a long time ago. Rachel had to nip to Boots to buy earplugs, as she was unable, she explained, to sleep on public transport at all. A rowdy group of men in tight-fitting shirts roared a drinking anthem through the building; two women in treacherously high stilettos, one wearing a pink sash that read 'Miss Chievous', were having a shouting match by the ticket machine. A young, black boy was being apprehended by several ticket inspectors for riding his electric scooter through the station. Tabitha watched, mesmerised by the goings-on of the crowd until Rachel reappeared with a bottle of orange juice, and Odilio hurried them to the platform.

They reached Edinburgh at four in the morning. Odilio awoke bleary-eyed, as the conductor's whistle blew several times from the platform, and the train doors opened, letting the freezing air raid the carriage's warmth. Despite securing the best accommodation on the train, he'd slept terribly. He ached all over and suspected he'd slept for little more than an hour. But he didn't care; this was part of the magic. A sense of excitement explained the sleeplessness, and in Odilio's experience, tiredness was a sort of stimulant. Tiredness made the brain work differently: it alerted one to their surroundings in a more primal way. They wheeled their suitcases from the station to the parking bay, where Phillip's driver was waiting for them. They filled the boot with luggage, clambered into the vehicle and slept for the drive to Aviemore. It was daylight when they arrived.

"Bring it in, old boy, bring it in," Phillip chuckled as they embraced in the driveway of the old manor house. A light rain had started to fall and a member of Phillip's staff was holding an umbrella for them to stand under.

"Good to see you," Odilio beamed. "It's been a while."

"You know you're always welcome."

"I know," said Odilio. "Well, we're here now."

The two men sized each other up for visible changes as people who haven't seen each other in a long time do. Phillip was lean with thin features. His crooked nose leant his face a rustic quality, like an old farmer's. Several inches taller than Odilio, he walked with a stoop that aged him slightly. Phillip was the only member of Helena's family that Odilio had ever felt completely accepted by. Their father was a hard, workaholic of a man; their mother, cold and distant. Odilio had always been seen as something of a mistake to the family — a notch down from what they felt their daughter deserved. That they'd recently settled in South Africa was convenient for everyone. Odilio only had to contend with a visit once every few

110

years. But Phillip had never joined in this conspiracy against him. He'd had his own issues in the past — his own brush with familial rejection — and on this they had common ground. They were similar in other respects. Both had a stiff air about them that was more a front than it was the person underneath. Like Odilio, Phillip was guarded in his expression of emotion. He maintained a poker face that only occasionally dropped to reveal the more eccentric character beneath. The two men shared a respectful bond that had been cemented on numerous trips to the estate.

The driver unloaded the car and hauled the luggage up to the entrance of the building. The manor house was a solid sandstone cube, with small, rectangular windows and a single, proliferating patch of ivy growing from the centre of its facade. It was details like the ivy, the embellishments around the window panes, and the decorative turrets on the four corners of the roof that lent the building the extent of its homeliness. Without these touches, the house would have looked like a psychiatric institution. There is a fine line between the antiquated and the depressing.

Tabitha joined her father under the umbrella. "Incredible," Phillip gushed, squatting to kiss his niece on the forehead. "You've gotten quite a bit taller," he said. "I remember you were this small when I last saw you." He bent down and held his hand inches from the floor. Tabitha laughed when she realised he was joking.

"And this is Rachel, Tabitha's au pair," said Odilio, gesturing to the figure racing from the car to the shelter of the umbrella.

"Hello!" Rachel cried as she struggled to pull the hood of her anorak over her head.

"A pleasure," Phillip saluted her.

"We have a tutor arriving tomorrow, too," said Odilio.

"How splendid," said Phillip. "The more the merrier. There's plenty of space, of course; it'll be good to blow the cobwebs off the guest rooms. Do you mind spiders, Tabitha?"

"I love them," she said.

"Good," he smiled. A droplet of rain dangled from the end of his nose. "There are lots of spiders here, so you'll be in good company. Right, I assume everyone is famished." He stood straight. "I've had the cooks prepare a proper Scotch breakfast. We'll eat up, then it's our first activity of the day. Salmon fishing. Have you ever done it, Tabitha? No? Well, you're in for a treat!"

The Glendales Estate — the house and surrounding land owned by Phillip Courtenay and his wife, Laurene — is a traditional 17th-century Scottish country estate, typical of the early classical period. The site contains over 15,000 acres of countryside and woodland. Phillip Courtenay purchased the property when he was alerted to its auction by a friend in the Scottish aristocracy. The house had fallen into disrepair following the imprisonment of its owner, jailed for a string of high-profile fraud cases. Phillip, whose family owned farmsteads in the southeast of England had fancied a go managing a genuinely rural piece of land and had snapped up the Glendales for a bargain. Laurene, his American wife, who never failed to mention her Scottish roots (nor her Czech, German, French or Irish ones, depending on the situation) had described a sense of homecoming when they secured the property. Fully refurbished at an undisclosed sum, it housed fifteen full-time members of staff, making a return for the family on its status as a hunting reserve: a corporate catering and accommodation bundle helped bulk out their income on this venture.

Rachel was shown to her bedroom in the building's eastern wing, where the staff lived. This area of the house was a 19th-century add-on. A fortune obtained in India had allowed the Glendales' owners to expand the land of the estate. New staff recruits had been necessary. The eastern wing was draughty and damp. Utilitarian rooms contained creaking beds acquired decades ago from a nearby nunnery. Odilio and Tabitha were led to the ballroom: the grand dining room cum highland spectacle, still panelled in the original 17th-century wood and decorated with portraits of the estate's former inhabitants. Wigged men in traditional dress posed contentedly beside their slaughtered quarry. In other paintings, dramatic landscapes set the scene for intense standoffs between highland creatures. The ballroom was reserved for customers and special guests: to rent it as part of a corporate bundle was an extra £10,000 per night. Tabitha held her uncle's hand as they made their way to the dining table at the end, where the staff were placing the last breakfast items down in trays. The smell of bacon filled the air. The family took their seats around the table. A rich spread of Scottish food had been laid out for them, and they eyed the various fixtures greedily.

"So, Tabitha," said Phillip, tucking his napkin into his shirt. "Your father tells me this will be your first time hunting. Are you excited?"

"Yes," she said, shyly. Her eyes were fixed on the pile of pancakes in front of her.

"Are you ready to catch your first fish? Shoot your first deer? Feast on its still-warm flesh?" Phillip grinned, revealing a mouthful of yellow teeth.

"Eww," said Tabitha. "I don't want to do that."

Odilio chuckled. "That's what we're here to change."

"It's going to be a laugh, Tabitha," Phillip grinned mischievously. "Back when there weren't any children to ruin the fun, we had a wild time here. Our nickname for your father was The Hyena: there wasn't a single part of an animal he wouldn't eat. You remember, Odilio? You used to fry deer hearts for breakfast."

"I remember," said Odilio. "They're full of good nutrition."

"That's disgusting," said Tabitha.

"Let's see if it runs in the family," Phillip laughed. "And how's work going?" He asked after some minutes of concentrated eating by the table.

Odilio was chewing a mouthful of black pudding. "Fine," he said, covering his mouth.

"I have your bit on The Lancaster half-read in my bathroom. I'm thoroughly enjoying it."

"Thanks," said Odilio. "It was a sitting duck, really."

"I could tell. They don't make it easy on themselves, do they? Those crusties, I mean. If they just scrubbed up a little and got themselves a haircut... And those tattoos! All credibility is tossed out the window when your arm looks like it's been attacked by a biro-wielding maniac. Tabitha, you're not going to become a crusty are you?" Tabitha shook her head as she chewed on a mouthful of syrupy pancakes. "Good," said Phillip. "A week in Aviemore will soon see to that." He finished his coffee, slamming the mug down on the table. "How's my lovely sister, anyway?" He looked at Odilio. "I hear she's arriving in a couple of days."

Odilio nodded. "Helena's at the Walkers' place in France. You remember Elizabeth?"

"Of course, I do," said Phillip.

"She's got a new artist under her wing. Showing him off to Sylvie down there."

"Helena mentioned," Phillip leant back in his chair and patted his stomach. "Sylvie Dupont? My wife was at a party with her recently. They have mutuals with the Beaumonts. Small world, isn't it?"

"Tiny," Odilio laughed.

"It won't be hard to squeeze her for a pretty penny. But it baffles and impresses me in equal measure how much my sister enjoys work. That never rubbed off on me," he chuckled.

The door of the dining hall creaked open, and Rachel appeared, accompanied by a member of the kitchen staff. "Sorry, I couldn't find you," she said. "I'm all unpacked."

"Come and get stuck in," said Odilio, gesturing to the remainder of food on the table. "I have to confess, we started without you."

"That's fine," she smiled.

"It's a maze, this place," said Phillip, pulling out a chair for her. "I don't suspect you'll know your way around any better by the end of the week. I still get lost from time to time. Help yourself." He passed her a plate of black pudding. "And how are you with a rifle, if you don't mind me asking? Ever nabbed a trophy?"

"A trophy?"

"Shot an animal," said Odilio.

"Oh, I haven't done anything like that," Rachel blushed. "I imagine I'd be quite useless, actually."

"Pity," said Phillip. "But nothing we can't work on."

She took a sip of coffee and buttered a slice of toast. "This looks delicious. Thanks so much for having me."

"Oh, *thank you.* We love having guests at the Glendales. I get bored otherwise."

"What do you do, if you don't mind me asking?" Rachel said, chewing on her toast.

"Bloody nothing," Phillip laughed. "Well, I run the estate, I guess that's something. But what it really involves is bossing around people who actually know what they're doing. My wife manages our investments — they seem to keep us sorted."

"Laurene's in Panama?" Odilio interrupted.

"That's right. Dreadful accounting mess. She won't be back for a while."

Phillip had met Laurene some years ago in London. Their relationship in its early stages was tumultuous to say the least. Phillip had been at pains to commit: he'd gone back and forth with a number of women, his erraticness exacerbated by his heavy drinking that at one point threatened to push both his wife and family

116

away for good. Then they bought the Glendales together. Phillip found peace away from the temptations of city life. They married and, soon afterwards, moved to Aviemore on a permanent basis. Just as Phillip's life was coming together, just as he was beginning to find his calling in the Scottish wilderness, Laurene took some time away for herself in the US. There were whisperings of a divorce. Phillip resorted to drinking again whilst his father hired a private investigator to accrue evidence of infidelity on his daughter-in-law's part. Nothing had been forthcoming, but the suspicion lingered following her return to Aviemore. In the meantime, Phillip managed to piece himself together again. Sobriety and therapy had kept things in place. Laurene was said to be happier these days, too.

Odilio's phone rang. "Excuse me," he said, standing up from the table. "It's work." He answered the phone in the hallway. "Cooper?"

"Odilio, you old dog. How is Scotland?"

"Everything's great," said Odilio.

"Glad to hear. I've just left a shareholder meeting. We're getting heat over our expenses, which is funny because I just okayed your next job to Amy — a pricey spot near where you're staying. Please do the business up there. I need everyone to pull something special out of the bag this week: they'll go through the next edition with a fine-tooth comb. I need your best work. Amy will send through the details. Is that okay?"

"That's fine," Odilio said.

"Oh, and we're getting shit over the Romano story. The shareholders are worried your links to him are giving us a bad image. I don't know what you're thinking, but I've said you've got nothing to do with it, so just stay out of it, okay?"

"I am out of it."

"Good. Then stay staying out of it — it's not worth getting wrapped up in all this. We need content. Good content: that's what our readers are interested in. Remember our chat? Keep it spicy. Okay, good, got to go. Send my love to Helena. Bye-bye."

An email notification buzzed on his phone. It was from Amy: 'Fwd: Reservation @ The Blue Langoustine.' He looked at his phone with contempt. He'd put Tony out of his mind since arriving in Scotland, but Phones were a portal into the bad and stressful. What had once been an innocuous novelty, a tool slightly more convenient than the corded landline now represented a gateway into bad news. He would have turned it off for the week if he could but reminded himself it would be wise to stay in contact with Helena until she arrived.

18

It was chucking it down as they drove to the river. Tabitha was looking out the window of the Land Rover as it struggled along the makeshift road that ran through the back of the Glendales. She watched the rolling hills unfold, bare of trees or even the smallest shrubs. A grass desert stretched out in every direction. The vehicle bobbed up and down on the ruts of the dirt track. "Don't worry about that, Tabitha," said Odilio, turning to his daughter in the backseat. "Phillip has the best waterproofs in the business: a little rain won't hurt us. Anyway, we're wading in the river. Might as well embrace it. You love salmon, don't you?"

"Yes," said Tabitha.

"Good, because we're going to eat plenty of it tonight."

The wind came in pulses across the valley, rippling through the grass in waves before breaking at the hill peaks, spraying water into the air like crashing tides. "Let's hope Tabitha doesn't get all vegetarian on us," Odilio said. "Did I tell you she has a vegetarian tutor, Phil?"

"Does she really?" said Phillip, his eyes on the road. "It seems to be all the rage, suddenly."

"You're telling me," said Odilio, who was filling his pipe with tobacco. In the highlands, he allowed himself the pleasure of the occasional smoke. The coarse blend of cherry and vanilla tobacco had been recommended by his brother-in-law. "I've been trying to warn everyone for years," he added.

"Is this true, Tabitha: your tutor is a vegetarian?" Phillip glanced in the mirror.

"Yes," said Tabitha.

"And he's coming *here*?" Phillip furrowed his eyebrows in mock fury. "Back in his glory days, your father wouldn't let a veggie within five hundred yards of the house. Now he has one teaching his daughter." He turned to Odilio and laughed. "That is funny. I wonder if I could get a hundred quid from The Sun for that information?"

Glory days, Odilio thought. The casualness of the remark stung more than he expected. He lit a match and held it to the pipe bowl, taking a big draw to light the tobacco. He blew the smoke out through a gap in the window. "Well, it makes no difference to Tabitha," said Odilio. "She's going to show what a natural-born hunter she is — aren't you, Tabs?" He turned around to look at her again. "Ey? Uncle Phillip won't tease us when he sees the size of the salmon we're about to catch." In the backseat, Tabitha was drawing figures in the window condensation with her finger.

They pulled up by the river. Under the shelter of the boot, they dressed in their waterproofs and waders, and then followed Phillip to the edge of the water. The river was flowing rapidly. The banks had been eroded to smooth planes of mud; what was carried away by the current gave the river the appearance of a chocolate milk chute. "The salmon pools spread wider here; they're spooked easily," Phillip whispered. "We want to wade in as little as we can, just enough to secure an anchor point." Odilio and Phillip carried the two fly-fishing rods. Tabitha held the landing

120

net. "Down there," said Phillip, pointing to a bend in the river with a rocky inlet. "It's fuller, that bit; there's a good chance of a catch. You and Tabitha can take it from there; I'll set up here."

Odilio waded a few steps into the water, holding Tabitha's hand, who followed him in. The water was up to her waist in her wading outfit. Odilio wore long wellington boots with gaiters that reached his crotch. The rain was pelting down, and he adjusted his waterproof toggles to keep it from getting into his hood. "Right, darling, this is a fly fishing rod," said Odilio. Tabitha clung to her hat as her father checked the equipment. She grimaced as the gale-force winds pummelled her back. "It's not like traditional fishing," he shouted, "where we weigh the end of the line so it sinks to the bottom. With fly fishing, we want our bait to sit on top of the water. The line is weighted so we can cast it, but we don't want the bait itself to sink." A burst of hail lashed down on them. Tabitha cried out as pieces of ice caught her face. "Listen carefully," Odilio yelled. "We want the fish to think a fly has landed on the surface of the river. Now, it has to go really far because we don't want them to hear or smell us. Let me show you."

He readied the line. Odilio hadn't fly-fished in a long time. The technique had always been somewhat elusive to him. He tended to cast like a lure fisher, whereas the correct technique for a fly was a sort of whip-like stroke that made the line unfurl mid-air. His first attempt ended badly; the line slapped the water's surface in front of him. He tried again, successfully. "See, like that," he turned to Tabitha. "Now, give it a few minutes to see if anything bites: if not, we do it again. Notice the orange colour of the line is there to attract the fish to the surface."

121

"They think it's a big worm," said Tabitha, through chattering teeth.

"What?" Odilio shouted, who could hear nothing over the wind.

"The fish think it's a big worm," she repeated.

"Exactly," said Odilio, who still could not hear her.

Upstream, Phillip was casting with a proficiency that made Odilio's attempts look poor. There was a rhythm to the way he moved the line through the air; the duration he left the fly on the water before reeling it in and trying again. He moved like a clockwork toy, his entire body involved, except his eyes that remained fixed on the water's surface. He was lost in the fishing. The wind and hail didn't bother him at all.

"Maybe they're not coming because it's raining," Tabitha said, pulling on her father's arm. Odilio, who had just failed another cast, reeled the line in impatiently. He stole glances at his brother-in-law to see what his technique was missing. His hands were numb from the cold, but it was impossible to do what he needed to do in gloves. He cast out again, further than his other attempts, but the line slapped the water's surface, and he knew the cast was not good. He thought about moving to another area of the river. "What was that, darling?" he said.

"Maybe," said Tabitha, trying to project her voice against the oncoming wind, "they're not biting because it's raining."

"Don't be silly, darling," Odilio said. "The salmon live in water, don't they? Why would they care about a spot of rain?"

"But how can they see the fly if there are millions of raindrops?"

122

Odilio stopped what he was doing as he considered the point. "Phillip?" he shouted down the river.

"Aye?" Phillip shouted back.

"Phillip, does this work in the rain? I mean, will they see the flies, the fish?"

"Oh, aye," Philip yelled. "The wiliest ones come out in the rain."

"See, it's fine," Odilio grunted.

"Can I have a go, please, Daddy?" Tabitha asked.

Tabitha's first cast was good, he had to give it to her. She was a natural at letting the line withdraw over her shoulder before whipping it forward at just the right time. Odilio suspected his ample experience in lure fishing actually impeded his ability to perform this motion correctly. Tabitha, unencumbered by the motor memory of a different action, took to the correct casting technique with ease. After a couple of attempts, she managed to impress Phillip enough to rouse him from his riverside meditation. "Very good, Tabitha!" he called over.

The sun broke through the clouds as the rain started to subside. The wind was calmer, and the feeling was beginning to return to Odilio's hands. He was impressed by his daughter's unfussedness at standing in a river in torrential rain; she'd taken to the task with enthusiasm, and he was happy to be spending time with her. It was the first time they'd done anything like this together, and Odilio reminded himself that such quality time was the original reason for their trip to Scotland.

Upstream, Phillip let out an enthusiastic ejection. He crouched, poised to resist the now taut line, then began to reel it in slowly. The tip of the rod jerked two or three times as the creature on the end resisted in pulses. "Need a hand?" Odilio cried out.

"Net," Phillip shouted, gesturing towards the bank. "Yaar, she's a beast."

Odilio skipped to the river bank, clambering up the slippery edge to fetch the net beside the fishing box. Tabitha remained in the water, watching her uncle struggle with the line. "Get over here," Phillip shouted at Odilio, who rushed to his side in the shallows. "Right, I'm going to back up the bank. She's too big to take out; I'll coax her into the net. As soon as she's in, whip her out and we'll de-hook. She's not going to hang around for long."

Phillip edged backwards, using his knees to gain traction on the bank. He wrenched the rod upwards, the end straining with the full force of the catch. Odilio could see it now visible in the clearer shallows. A massive, silvery fish: a fine specimen of Atlantic salmon. "Look, Tabitha! Come here!" he shouted, preparing the net to swipe the creature out of the water. Tabitha bolted forward: in the rush, she lost her footing on a rock. She screamed as she tripped into the freezing water. "Come on, come on, Tabitha," Odilio shouted. He was not feeling sympathetic and knew if they landed the fish, they would all be in a similar nick — Phillip was already caked in a layer of mud as he shimmied up the river bank.

Tabitha was fighting back tears when she reached her father. "Do you see it?" he said. She nodded. There was a blue tint to her lips. "Right," he said. "Hold me in case I fall." She grabbed a crease in his raincoat and held on. The fish was

124

thrashing about in the shallows; a foam had formed around its tail where it frothed up the surface of the water. Poised with the net, Odilio shovelled it out of the river in one purposeful manoeuvre. The fish writhed around in the air. "Good work!" Phillip cried from the river bank.

"What a beauty," Odilio said, inspecting the net's contents, before bounding for dry land. Tabitha was almost dragged into the river again before she remembered to let go.

Odilio laid the fish down on the grass. Phillip took the de-hooker from the toolbox and removed the hook from the salmon's mouth while Odilio held it in place. "She's about thirty pounds," said Odilio, inspecting it.

"Easily," said Phillip. "Thirty-five, I'd say. Come and have a look, Tabitha." Tabitha approached cautiously. The fish flailed around with more physicality than she would have imagined. It seemed to be constituted wholly of muscle, and she wondered if it wouldn't stop trashing until it was back in the water.

Phillip took another tool from the box. It looked like a miniature baseball bat. "What's that?" Tabitha asked, aware of a shift in her uncle's demeanour.

"This is a poacher's priest," he said, holding it up. "We use it to give the last rites to the animal."

"We use it to beat the fish's brain out," Odilio guffawed.

"You could put it like that," said Phillip. "See, it's significantly less humane to leave it here suffocating."

"It would be here for an hour if we didn't," Odilio added, this time seriously.

"Right, who's going to do the job?" The two men looked at each other. They looked at Tabitha. "Are you going to do it, my Tabby cat?"

Tabitha stared at the salmon flailing around on the floor. The thrill of catching it — watching the two adults howl like children — had suddenly disappeared. She was feeling very cold. "Go on, Tabs," said Odilio. "Do it for me." Tabitha said nothing. A single fish eye stared at her from the grass. The circularity of the eye gave the face a surprised look. She did not want to hit the eye with the poacher's priest. She wanted to return the fish to the water and then go home.

"I clubbed a trout at your age," said Odilio. "It's quick then it's over. The fish feels nothing. Then we can go home and eat it."

"She'll feed the entire house," said Phillip. "The servants will go hungry otherwise." He leaned forward and pressed the priest into her hand.

"Go on, darling," said Odilio. "A quick whack on the head, then we're finished."

Tabitha chewed on a fingernail. She watched as the animal struggled on the floor. "No, I don't want to," she said.

"Come on, Tabitha," Odilio said, this time more sternly. "Do it, please."

"Go on," said Phillip. "At least give it a go."

Tabitha shook her head.

"But it's why we're here!" said Odilio. "It's a hunting weekend: this is what it means to hunt. Now hit it quickly; you're putting it in *more* misery by wasting time."

Tabitha dropped the priest. "I don't want to," she said.

"For Christ's sake," Odilio muttered. He took the priest from the floor. "Shall I do the honours, Phil?" He turned to his brother-in-law and smiled, trying to rekindle an earlier jovialness.

"One of us has to," said Phillip. "Thank you."

The priest came down hard on the fish's head. Odilio pulled back and watched the creature as it thrashed around with renewed urgency. A strange hissing sound came from somewhere within its body: an unnerving scream he did not know fish were capable of producing. Nothing, otherwise, changed in its appearance. He swung again, slamming down the club with even greater force, but still, nothing indicated it was on its way out. He swung again and again; Odilio was starting to panic. Only on the fifth or sixth go did the first signs of injury reveal themselves, yet the fish only continued in its struggle. Ten, eleven strikes, and an eyeball popped out. Blood splattered from its broken head on each stroke of the mallet. The others watched in horror. Odilio was breathing heavily. He desperately wanted it over. The fish sounds were becoming increasingly gargled the more it was beaten. A bloody mist stained his coat.

"Give it here," said Phillip, snatching the club from him. He struck with an accuracy that put the fish to rest immediately. It thrashed no more. "You need to dislodge the spine from its head," he said calmly, wiping blood from the priest with his handkerchief. "Christ, you've made a mess of it." Both eyeballs littered the grass. A clear fluid seeped from the fish's broken skull. "Well, it's not photogenic, but it'll cook a treat. Let's get it in the car." Odilio glanced briefly at his daughter and fancied he saw hatred in her eyes. She said nothing on the drive to the house

127

and went straight to her room as soon as they got in. The late afternoon sun was breaking through the clouds and it had finally stopped raining.

19

"One quick drink before the gate?"

"There isn't time for a drink."

"There's always time for a quick drink," Elias said, rooting himself in the middle of the busy throughway. "We're first-class passengers, and they've got our bags in hold. They *have to* wait for us."

Helena checked her watch. "Take off is in fifteen minutes," she said, shooing him onwards.

"They'll call our names a hundred times before that plane goes anywhere," Elias pleaded, eyeing up the bar.

Helena looked at him with a mixture of pity and resentment. "Knock yourself out, then," she said, parking her wheelie case by her feet. They were standing beside The Heathrow Airport Oyster & Champagne Bar on their way to the gate for a flight advertised as 'boarding: final call'.

Elias smirked. He looked over at the stand with its solitary client nursing a champagne flute and several empty mollusc shells. "I don't want a drink, actually," he said.

"Good," said Helena, as they continued to the gate in silence.

This was the second attempt at making it to Antibes that day. The 8 am flight was perhaps overly ambitious. Helena had made it; Elias had not. Forty missed calls had failed to rouse him into action. There'd been no word from her protege until after midday. Hours of pacing the departures lounge, calling everyone she could think of to locate her missing artist while ensuring she maintained a professional image at all times. Chalk it up as a miscommunication, a crossing of wires. Did anyone know where he was? You can never get hold of artists — they're always so absorbed in everything! Meanwhile, Elias had been smoking PCP in a flat in Hackney, having failed to notice the sun was up. He'd arrived at the airport, nine hours late, wearing a crumpled Burberry suit, carrying only a painting rolled into a cardboard tube for luggage (not even a toothbrush!). Helena had resisted the urge to lash out. Instead, she tried to play it cool. "Where's your luggage?" she'd asked. He shrugged at her. He reeked of stale cigarette smoke. His face was drawn and tired-looking. "You haven't brought anything with you? Not even a phone charger or hairbrush?" He'd grinned stupidly. "You don't even think to take a pen and paper?"

"Chill," he slurred with the intonation of a drunk person trying to sound sober.

"If the Walkers see you like this, they'll kick you out of their house."

Elias blinked slowly. "You didn't say they were such stiffs, *man*." He laughed to himself as if lost in the fragments of a joke from the previous evening. "Come on, let's go to fucking France!" he shouted across the departures lounge.

Now, they were on the plane, waiting to take off for the Cote D'Azur. Elias was returning to earth; a horrid anxiety was creeping in as the drugs were wearing off. Only the sensation of Helena's body against his could make him feel better now. He sidled up to her in his seat, relaying the contents of his thoughts as they came to him: how making art was something he'd done to sound legitimate after

130

flunking university. Something to make him feel less useless living off his mother's ample allowance… A ruse to get women in the sack, for which he'd been phenomenally successful. Was he being too forward? "I'm a fraud," he said, bringing it back a little. "I'm not who you think I am." He leant in close telling her this, his eye-contact unflinching. Would she make the first move? Would she try to get off with him? "I guess I'm just Ingrid's idiot son to you," he put his head in his hands. "If only you trusted me, you'd see what I was capable of."

Helena took a deep breath, forcing an amicable expression. "I only see you as a child if you behave like one," she said, concessively. "You need to keep it together. Sylvie Dupont is not going to have my level of patience. You know, I think she owns a portion of this airline. She's doing us a huge favour meeting us this weekend. If we slip up, we won't get a second chance." Helena was reassured by the idea that, short of having smuggled anything onto the plane, he would have to remain sober for the weekend ahead. She put her hand on his knee for a brief second. "So just do your best to behave. I know you're brimming with ideas, and this isn't what interests you, but do it properly now and then we can do whatever we need to do afterwards. How does that sound?"

"It sounds fair," he swallowed. Helena raised the partition between their seats, put on her eye mask and fell asleep. Elias ordered a bottle of champagne from the dining cart, which he drank alone whilst watching Iron Man 2 on the in-flight entertainment system.

20

"Perfect," said Phillip, tending to the fire with his poker. "What a marvellous afternoon." On the armchair beside him, Tabitha was sitting on Rachel's lap. They were sticking stickers in a sticker book. It was six o'clock and dark outside. Rain pelted the windows of the old room. The shutters rattled in the wind, but inside, the air was smokey and still. The fire roared in the stone hearth, filling the room with cosy orange light.

Odilio brought in a tray of tin-foil-wrapped parcels and placed them next to the fire. "The salmon," he announced proudly, rubbing his hands together. Phillip positioned them carefully on the embers. "The best way to do salmon," Odilio continued. "A bit of sage and garlic; some sliced chilli and ginger. You don't need any oil; there's enough fat in the flesh. I leave the skin on, but Helena hates it. It's glorious when it goes nice and crisp." He poured himself some wine from the carafe and sat on the floor. "I'm looking forward to this. Tabitha, are you excited to eat the salmon we caught?" Tabitha, who was concentrating on her sticker book, said nothing. "What a luxury it is to catch our own fish and eat it the same day."

Phillip stoked the embers. The fire was really going. Odilio closed his eyes as a flush of tiredness spread through him. His cheeks were rosy from the contrast between the warm room and biting weather he'd spent the afternoon in.

Odilio opened his eyes. Philip was clawing frantically for the salmon parcels. "Everything okay?" asked Odilio.

"I think the fire's too hot." He launched a parcel onto the floor with the poker, blew on it several times, then prised the tinfoil open with his fingertips. The flesh was dark and dry. "Christ, it's buggered," he said, retrieving the other packages from the flames. "They're all ruined," Phillip moaned, glowering at the embers. "I didn't realise it was so hot; ten minutes is usually perfect."

"I'm sure we can eat around the burnt bits," said Odilio, with the disorientation of someone who has just woken from a nap.

They ate dinner around the fire, the flames crackling in the hearth, ejecting the occasional splinter with a pop. "It's very good," said Rachel, gnawing on her fillet. "Well done all of you for catching it!"

Odilio picked at the dry, tasteless flesh, a pile of bones and burnt debris amassing on the side of his plate. It seemed there was more debris than there had originally been fish.

"It's got so many bones," said Tabitha, scowling. It had an unforgivable number of bones given its size, Odilio thought. Phillip had done a terrible job filleting it.

A young Scottish lad — one of Phillip's kitchen staff — poked his head into the room. "Would anyone like pasta?" He asked.

"No," Odilio snapped.

"Yes, please!" said Tabitha.

"Finish your fish, first," said Odilio. "If you're hungry afterwards, then you can have pasta." Tabitha prodded the fillet with the tip of her fork.

"We're good, thank you," said Phillip, dismissing the cook.

133

"You know, Helena wanted to bring Maria along?" said Odilio. "I had to talk her out of it: there'd be more cooks than guests. Apparently, your father never travelled without his chef. It's a habit she picked up off of him."

Phillip laughed. "Agu was a dreadful cook but a lovely man. To be fair, he knew a million ways to prepare a potato. Dad was always happy."

"My mum cooked everything," said Odilio. "Wouldn't let dad near the kitchen. She never liked potatoes, funnily enough. Said they weren't worth the hassle." Odilio could still picture their kitchen in Oban, the windows steamed with traces of conversation and the cooking pot as a dense gravy rolled away on the stove.

"Oh, I love a good jacket potato," said Rachel. "You love potatoes, don't you, Tabitha?"

Tabitha didn't reply. She looked at the au pair in panic. Only when the same look was returned did she try to rectify the situation, letting out a retching noise that started in her lungs and ended abruptly in her throat, gaining the attention of her father and uncle.

"Tabitha's choking!" Rachel cried. Odilio and Phillip lurched towards her, but the au pair was there first. She forced her hand down her throat in time to dislodge a large fish bone and accompanying lump of regurgitated flesh. Tabitha let out several deep breaths as soon as she was able to.

"Jesus, Tabitha," said Odilio, "Why didn't you say something earlier?" He looked to his brother-in-law, then, to the shocked au pair, gauging their reactions to in turn ascertain the seriousness of the situation, or what could have been.

134

Phillip chuckled. "Could have been nasty," he said.

Rachel hugged Tabitha. "Are you okay?" she asked, her voice faintly trembling.

"I'm fine," sniffed Tabitha, who was in a state of embarrassed shock. "I hate fish; I want pasta," she said, opting to deflect the nervous attention that might otherwise make her cry.

"Declan!" Phillip called back for his cook. "Make up a big bowl of pasta, will you?"

*

Tabitha was in bed. Phillip had retired to his study. Odilio was by the fire, drinking his way through the last of the carafe. He'd found the wifi password on the router and scrolled, now, through his emails with tipsy indifference. There was the usual nonsense vying for his attention. A chocolate shop in Hampstead invited him to give a talk for its launch, offering to compensate him with a month's unlimited hot chocolate. DELETE. A fish and chip shop in Hoxton was shooting a documentary on its 100-year-old beer batter recipe and wanted Odilio as a talking head. SAVE FOR LATER. There was a legal notice from GALAXIAS informing him he was banned from the restaurant, including all those run by its parent company, Imperial Mollusc. No love lost, thought Odilio, placing it in his archive.

He was about to go to bed, when he received a WhatsApp message from Cooper. It was a link to an article in the Daily Mail. He clicked it, eyes peeled as he beheld the headline: RESTAURANT CRITIC ODILIO DEFENDS PERVERT ROMANO. He read in horror:

135

In the latest twist of the scandal surrounding disgraced TV chef Tony Romano, The Gent's senior restaurant critic, Odilio Brimble, has come out in support of his former colleague. Sources close to Mr Brimble suggest his sympathies lie with the ousted pervert, who he believes has done nothing wrong and is, instead, the victim of a social media 'witch hunt'. Photos of them sharing drinks at the Groucho would appear to corroborate these claims. Indeed, Odilio looked to be in good spirits, laughing and joking with his friend throughout the evening as they shared several drinks...

He scrolled through the dozen photos of their evening together, each one captioned with speculations on the content of their conversation. At the bottom of the page was a clip from their show. Odilio pressed play. It was of him and Tony, sitting on a beach somewhere along the Jurassic Coast. Tony was filleting a pile of freshly-caught mackerel as Odilio watched. There were numerous segments like this on 'The Critic and the Cook' — cooking pieces in which Tony put together dinner in the middle of nowhere, Odilio all the while grumbling that there wasn't a high-end restaurant around for miles (the reality was a scene like this could take several hours and a team of runners to prepare; Tony hated these set pieces even more than Odilio). Fresh mackerel boiled in a bucket of seawater, served with a paste of fresh herbs. They were dressed to accentuate the rather laboured dynamic between them: Odilio's linen shirt and cashmere scarf flailed in the sea breeze — the burgundy corduroys he didn't want to wet on the shingle, imparted, visually, his uselessness, while the stocky Sicilian got his hands dirty putting together a rustic, hearty supper on the beach.

136

"Filleting fish is like undressing a woman," Tony remarks, holding aloft his bloody knife. "You get more out of them when you're gentle." He throws a finished mackerel into the bucket on top of a dozen more. Odilio looks at him with an awkward smirk that seems to say: "Oh, *Tony*. Where are you going with this?"

"You really don't want to use a knife... but if you have to, be careful." He chuckles. "Best you don't cut yourself in the process."

He had a new message from Cooper. 'Not a good look.'

'Tabloid bullshit, Cooper,' Odilio replied.

'Well, it's you in the photos. I said stay out of it.'

'That was last week,' said Odilio. 'I told him his behaviour was unacceptable.'

'Well, you fucked it,' Cooper replied.

Odilio clicked back to the article. It wasn't a good look. Scanning the text, the words 'pervert', 'sex pest', 'disgraced', and 'toxic work environment', leapt out at him. There were already hundreds of comments — the website's thumbs up/thumbs down tool allowed him to gauge consensus on a whole different level.

'I thought Mr Brimble had more class than this, supporting that discusting man.' 115 thumbs up, 24 thumbs down.

'Greasy italian sleaze ball, no wonder they used to call him Mr Octopus at Porco.' 99 thumbs up, 4 thumbs down.

'Nothing surprises me. The establishment really are a bunch of pedos. Heads on pikes!' 409 thumbs up, 3 thumbs down.

Odilio was back on WhatsApp. 'What should I do?'

There was a pause before his editor replied: 'Ignore. Make the next piece big. Get everyone talking about that.'

'Will do,' Odilio replied.

He put down his phone and rolled over on the sofa. He closed his eyes. Within minutes he had drifted asleep, his head back on the sofa, gently snoring as he dreamt of deer — Highland red deer — charging across the grassy plains of rural Scotland. Their movements were synchronised and intentional, and they ran through the brooks as they ran through the heather, and they never stopped. The wilderness stretched endlessly ahead of them — theirs was the simple yet futile task to see it all. Odilio woke two hours later, with the fire having gone out, the room cold, his mouth caramelised with the lingering taste of red wine.

21

By Sunday morning the weather had turned pleasant. The sky was clear: a gold light imbued the surroundings with a quality unique to the season. Tree debris littered the grounds, testifying to the recent strong winds, but a stillness in the air promised a return to calm. The tutor arrived early that morning. He stepped onto the drive carrying a single holdall, breathing in the fresh autumnal decay. A member of Phillip's staff collected his bags from the car, then showed him to his room. Afterwards, they led him across the house to the orangery, where the family was sitting for breakfast.

"Stuart," Odilio said, noticing him enter. "You've made it in one piece."

"Just about," the tutor smiled. "What a night," he said, removing his coat.

"First time riding in a sleeper?" Phillip stood and proffered a hand to the young man.

"First in a long time," said the tutor. "You get used to it, backpacking, but this one came as a surprise."

"Phillip," said Phillip.

"Stuart, nice to meet you." They shook hands, and Phillip pulled up a chair.

"Will you take some coffee?" Odilio gestured to the cafetiere.

"Please," said the tutor. He sat down as Odilio filled his cup with a filter coffee as dark as marmite. "Milk?"

"Black, please," said the tutor.

"Of course," Odilio smiled. "Sugar?"

"No, thank you."

"As you wish," Odilio placed the cup next to him. The tutor drank immediately. By the stove in the corner, Rachel and Tabitha were playing a board game.

"Hi, Stuart," Rachel waved at him with a smile. They were playing the board game version of Minecraft: it had been Helena's idea to buy board game versions of video games that Tabitha had heard about from older children. It stalled the inevitable clashes they would soon have over computer use. The 'trick' worked, and the board games, for now, satisfied their daughter's curiosity. Tabitha looked up from the board and Stuart waved at her. "Hello Tabitha," he said.

"Hello," she replied, glancing at him shyly.

"I have a lunch assignment," Odilio announced to the room. "It's on the other side of the loch. For work: I'm taking Phillip with me. What's the plan here?"

The tutor sipped his coffee. "I'm happy to get started whenever," he said. "How are you, Tabs? Ready for a lesson?"

"What's a loch?" said Tabitha, looking at her father.

"It's like a lake," said Rachel.

"It's exactly a lake," said Phillip.

"It's Gaelic for the very same thing," said Odilio, who was buttering a croissant. "It's a cognate with Manx, Cornish, and one of the Welsh words, 'llwch', I think."

140

"It's like padlock," said Tabitha.

"No," said Odilio.

"They say there's a big serpent in the loch, don't they?" Rachel grinned, directing the comment to Tabitha. "It eats children, or so I've heard."

"It *doesn't,*" Tabitha rejoined. Her tone invited Rachel to tell her more.

"That's Loch Ness," Odilio interrupted. "This is Loch Morlich. The only thing in there is salmon. It's children who eat those."

"Which reminds me," said Phillip, looking up from his plate, to the tutor. "I've been told you have certain dietary requirements, is that correct?"

"Yes," Stuart nodded. "I'm vegan."

"Splendid," said Phillip. "Bit of a silly question, but that does quite rule out chicken, doesn't it?"

"Unfortunately, it does," said the tutor.

"Cheese, no? Eggs as well?"

"No dairy, really."

"Great," said Phillip. "I'll have a word with my cooks. We'll sort you out, no problem."

"Thank you."

Odilio dropped his napkin onto his plate. "I should get ready. Might be gone a while. Stuart, when you've finished your class, maybe you and Rachel could take Tabitha on a walk? There are some splendid routes around the glen, here."

"Sure," said the tutor, his eyes wondering across the room, back to Rachel. "It's such a lovely day."

22

The Blue Langoustine sits on the eastern shore of Loch Morlich. A small, ramshackle cottage: the rustic, old-world facade conceals its otherwise opulent interiors. The Blue Langoustine is a three-Michelin-star classic. People come from all over the world to sample its legendary fusion food, where French methods of seafood preparation rub shoulders with British offal classics. For Odilio, a visit to The Blue Langoustine was long overdue. Colleagues had declared it the finest establishment north of the border. Stepping out of the Land Rover, his first impression was how much smaller it looked than in the photographs. It was a journalistic cliché to describe a place as a Tardis, but looking at that stocky stone cottage, not much bigger than a highland bothy, it was difficult to believe any food — much less of a Michelin-star quality — could be prepared inside. "This is going to be good," said Odilio. The Blue Langoustine was the perfect springboard for a 1200-word bit of carnivorous propaganda. He was on home turf in a place like this. He only had to show up and show off a little.

"Good afternoon, Sirs," the maître d' greeted them at the door.

"Table for two: Le Foie," Odilio said. Through a gap in the curtain that partitioned the dining room from the tiny foyer, Odilio could see into the bustling restaurant. A few packed tables delivered the soundscape of an ordinary establishment: the chitter-chatter of diners and scraping of cutlery on plates. There were more staff than customers. Michelin starred food — two Michelin stars in

142

particular — demanded perfection at every opportunity. You needed a small army to stay in business: a fleet of keen-eyed obsessives, ready to pounce on so much as a poorly placed sprig of parsley.

The maître d' skimmed through an iPad, searching for the reservation on a spreadsheet. "I can't see any tables for two," they said.

Odilio glanced at Phillip. "What about Le Foie? Eton Le Foie?"

The maître d' looked pensively at the tablet. "Wait… I have a table for three in that name. In fact, one of your party is already here."

"Really?"

"Sirs, table six. Come with me." They placed the iPad on the counter.

"Strange," whispered Phillip, as they were led to the dining room. Odilio didn't take in any details of the tables around him; his eyes followed the maître d' straight to their own. Shit. Oh, shit, he thought, registering the figure towards the back of the room. Oh, please, no.

"Surprise, surprise. Bet you didn't expect to find me here."

"I didn't," said Odilio. "Good to see you, Tony." His squat friend stood to squeeze him in a bear hug. His breath reeked of scotch and his body felt hot beneath his blue cotton shirt. "Good to see you, too," he patted Odilio firmly on the back. "Who's your friend?"

"This is Helena's brother, Phillip."

"Spitting image," Tony laughed at his half-formed joke. "Good to meet you."

"Actually, we've met before," said Phillip. "Odilio's fiftieth?"

143

Tony looked at him blankly.

"Monkey Island... Bray?"

"Lord knows if I remember anything from that weekend," Tony laughed again.

"I remember you well," said Phillip, with a hint of sorrow.

"Can I get you gentlemen a drink?" the waiter interrupted.

"Three large gin and tonics," said Tony.

"Just two," said Phillip. "And a lime soda."

"Very good," the waiter bowed out.

"You must be wondering what I'm doing here," said Tony with a grin.

"I'll admit, I am," Odilio said, checking the room for anyone vaguely resembling a reporter. *Stay out of it* — his editor's words resounded in him.

"Well, what are the chances? I have a place up this way, not far from Morlich. A little farm I bought years ago with that bitch, Jane. I've spent twenty years talking about doing it up. Never seemed to have a spare moment. Now, with all the nonsense in London, I've finally got my chance. Thought it'd be nice to get away for a bit. Didn't want to go *too far*, mind. Here's perfect. I'm hiding out if you like, which as it turns out, so are you!"

"I'm on holiday with the family," said Odilio "And I'm on a job right now." His voice trailed off. "I didn't know you lived near."

At once, Odilio realised this wasn't true. On many drunken evenings over the years, he'd heard Tony talk about his 'little place' in the Cairngorms. Like many details from those nights, they hadn't stuck — whether or not it was from

144

consuming a brain-stomping quantity of alcohol, or a lingering desire to forget as many details as possible, Odilio couldn't be sure. He kicked himself for the oversight. What rotten luck.

"Don't look so disappointed," Tony smirked as he scanned the room. "Not a bad assignment. This is one of my favourite places. The best thing to happen to Aviemore, maybe to the whole of Scotland."

"But how did you know we would be here?" Odilio asked. The waiter arrived with their drinks. Tony reached for his gin and tonic and grinned.

"My mate Jonny is the head chef. He gave me a bell, said he fancied you were coming. Eton Le Foie: that ridiculous pseudonym is as prolific as your real name in the trade. I told him I saw you in London last week. Said we'd had a lovely evening together. I thought I'd raise my head briefly from the trenches and pay you a visit. I asked him not to tell you; I wanted to keep it a surprise. He thought it would be a good laugh, too, so they added an extra chair to the table. So, surprise." He raised his drink for a toast. "To surprises." They clinked glasses. Tony turned to Phillip. "Has Odilio filled you in on what happened to me?"

"I read the newspapers," said Phillip, stirring his lime soda. "I'm aware."

"Bloody rotten luck, eh?" Tony shook his head. Phillip watched the bubbles in his glass stream to the surface. "Well, at least some friends have my back." He raised his drink and nodded to Odilio, who sat in dumbfounded contemplation. *Sources close to Mr Brimble suggest his sympathies lie with the ousted pervert.* It wouldn't take much for a PR team to pass themselves off as 'sources'. It was the kind of outlandish act of selfishness that Tony was capable of.

Was he being paranoid? Perhaps now wasn't the time to probe that question. He was here, on company money, on a special assignment he needed to get right. He'd deal with Tony later.

"Let's put that behind us," said Odilio. "For the sake of lunch."

"Good idea," Tony said, reaching for the menu. "I'm famished."

"Any recommendations? If you're a regular, I mean."

Tony cast his eyes on the menu with a hint of pride. "Let me start by swearing an oath of devotion to the lobster. The proper ones at the bottom here: the only ones worth eating. They catch it down the road. Small things, packed with flavour. The cheap stuff is bigger, but it tastes like water. I like to suck the tastiest morsels out of the shell, don't you?"

Odilio nodded. He studied the menu, noticing the prices weren't listed. The food was served by its weight in grams — a metric that eluded his common sense. "Of course, I couldn't let you leave without sampling the scallops. What are people's thoughts on offal?"

"I've always been a fan," said Odilio.

"Oh, I know *you* are," said Tony "You'd cannibalise a child if they'd let you." He raised an eyebrow to Phillip.

"Yes, count me in," Phillip said.

"Then we'll get some of the liver pate, as well as the mallard tongues on dripping toast. The skate cheeks are exquisite, and we could do worse than the tripe. Who likes sweetbreads?"

146

The others nodded unenthusiastically. "Then for the wines, I'm more than happy to do the pairings. We'll get the Sancerre for the fish, then a full-bodied Merlot for the meat. A round of scotches while we wait, of course."

"I don't drink," said Phillip. "So it might be worth going by the glass."

"Tripe," Tony grinned. "More for us, then," he winked at Odilio. The waiter arrived with his notebook. "Right, listen carefully," said Tony.

By the time the starters were cleared away, Tony was drunk. He had gone it alone on the scotch and had helped himself to most of the wine. Odilio nursed his glass of Sancerre, resisting numerous attempts to have it topped up. Tony had been effusive before the food had appeared. Now, he was indulging himself in a stream of conscious rambling, enlivened by the introduction of fuel into his system. Self-justifications found their way into every one of his anecdotes. He could jump from a nostalgic recounting of a childhood memory to decrying the evils of political correctness with a speed that defied logic. Odilio had tried to focus on the food, although he was beginning to feel like a used pair of ears. It didn't matter what you said to Tony; what counted was that you agreed with everything *he* said. Odilio had been unable to make a single interesting observation of the meal itself. The entire lunch was imbued with the sour tones of Tony Romano.

The main courses arrived. Three bright red lobsters were placed on the table along with tool kits to dissect their shells. Tony was a dab hand at collecting flesh from the exoskeleton. He talked non-stop as he forked lobster into his mouth, salvaging meat from the obscurest reaches of the shells. Odilio picked limply at the crustacean, his appetite having quickly left him. The rich smell of garlic butter and

147

seafood was making him nauseous. Phillip, too, struggled to manifest enthusiasm.
"Isn't it gorgeous?" said Tony, washing down a mouthful of lobster with a large
gulp of wine. "I've always said, a man who can eat shellfish properly is a man who
knows how to perform cunnilingus well." Odilio choked a little. He could feel his
stomach churn at the remark.

Tony was slurring by the time they finished the main courses. The table
was strewn with the waste of shellfish, calf innards, and a sickly rich plate of
porkish god-knows-what (the sweetbreads had followed the lobster; mountain
octopus, which was not on the menu, had been served compliments of the chef. It
was a dish of roasted pig's ears). It was late afternoon, and theirs was the only table
still in the restaurant. Tony was distributing the last dregs of red wine. "Not for me,"
said Odilio, as the bottleneck probed the rim of his glass. Tony ignored him and
emptied it. The waitress arrived to clear the plates. "Dessert?" she asked them.

"The bill, please, when you're ready," said Odilio, firmly.

"Sure thing," she replied. She was young, perhaps no older than twenty,
and spoke with a strong eastern European accent. Tony's eyes followed her as she
walked away from the table. It was a look Odilio was familiar with. "You see my
quandary," he said. His eyes were glistening from their sockets.

"What quandary?" asked Phillip.

Tony snorted. He looked over Phillip's shoulder and grinned. "Working
around an arse like that." He exhaled through his lips with the sound of a deflating
tyre. "What can a man do when he's got that in his face all day? Don't you just want

to bend it over and smash it? He knows what I mean." Tony beamed at Odilio, whose eyes found the floor.

Tony couldn't walk straight across the car park. He laughed as he fumbled in his pockets for his keys. "He obviously can't drive," Phillip muttered. Odilio grimaced as he watched Tony fall against his car. "Tony, why don't we call you a taxi?"

"You can call me what you like!" Tony burst out laughing.

"Let's drop you off in our car," said Odilio. "You're up the road, right?" His voice wobbled. He wanted to get rid of Tony as quickly as possible: he didn't care if the old meathead put himself out of his misery against a telegraph pole on the way home, but he'd never live with himself if he took someone else out on the way.

"I want to take my car," said Tony, holding up his keys.

"You're over the limit," said Odilio. "You're stinking drunk; you'll get arrested. Then you'll be in more trouble than you're already in." Tony glowered at Odilio, a brief second of confused rage. The age gap between the men — the fact that Tony had been successful before Odilio — meant, by some unwritten agreement, it was unforgivable for the younger to talk to his elder in a way that wasn't gushingly respectful.

Odilio knew in these moments that you had to give a little. He had to concede something to make Tony feel like he'd won. "Fine, we'll take your car," he said. "Philip can drive us to your place, then one of your men can drop us back here to get the Land Rover."

"Haven't got any staff," Tony hiccupped. "Left them in London. Don't want anyone around."

Odilio rubbed his cheeks. "Okay, Phillip, you take the Land Rover. I'll drive Tony in his car. I'm not sober, but I'm good to go."

Phillip nodded tersely. "Go slowly," he said: "I'll follow behind."

It was a short drive to Tony's house. Odilio took extra care handling the brand new sports car as gently as it could go. Every feature of its design seemed to only have speed in mind. Odilio placed the BMW M3 in a low gear, driving it like a golf cart along the winding road that ascended from the lake to the hill near where Tony lived. Meanwhile, he did his best to ignore his old friend's incessant relaying of details pertaining to the vehicle's performance capabilities: details regarding acceleration, fuel economy, horsepower, and so forth. The drive seemed to be sobering Tony up. It was almost refreshing hearing his old friend monologue about inline engines and live rear axles rather than his misgivings on modern feminism.

At the top of the hill, they turned into a lane that wound down to Tony's house. Below, in the next valley, Odilio could make out the stone cottage with its ancient barn. Even from a distance, there was a dilapidated look about the place. Rusting agricultural equipment was strewn across the ground, and only now, halfway down the lane, could Odilio make out the presence of four or five men in the drive. "Who are those people?" Odilio asked.

"Stop, stop!" Tony hissed. Odilio applied the brakes.

"Shit, it's them," said Tony.

"Press?" asked Odilio.

"Worse," said Tony. "Fucking creditors. I owe a fair bit of money. Some of the early venture capital for my business was in company bonds. A great deal for them: tripled their investments. Fuckers had plenty of time to cash in. Turn around. I can't see them now."

"I can't," said Odilio.

"Why not?" Tony snapped.

"I can't turn around here. The road's as wide as the car, and I don't fancy falling down there." He glanced at the drop that descended to the next turn of the lane thirty feet below.

"Give it here," Tony said, undoing his seatbelt.

"Not a chance," said Odilio. "You'll kill us."

Behind them, in the Land Rover, Phillip bibbed his horn. "Idiot," Tony spat. "They'll see us; we've got to reverse." Odilio turned in his seat and looked out the rear window. He gestured to Phillip to go back.

It took five minutes for both vehicles to reverse up the track. Further down the main road, out of view of the house, they pulled into a layby. "What happened?" Phillip asked, winding down his window. "Wrong turn?"

"Tony's creditors are down there. He says he can't go back."

"They'll kill me," said Tony in a self-pitying voice from the passenger seat.

"Right," said Phillip. "What do you want to do, then? There's a hotel in Aviemore which is quite decent." Odilio turned to Tony, waiting for him to say something.

"Whatever," said Tony. "Look, take me to yours, and we can make a plan from there. I'm shaken up and need to get my head together."

"I guess we could stop off at yours?" Odilio looked guiltily at his brother-in-law.

"I guess we could," Phillip said, winding up the window.

"Thanks for this," said Tony as they drove to the estate. The sun was setting over the mountains. A pink light beamed through the windscreen. Odilio said nothing as they tailed Phillip's car. His focus was on the road ahead. He was thinking, too, and his thoughts ranged wildly in their appetite for violence. One minute, he imagined booting Tony out of the car, reversing it over him, before fleeing the country. The next, he felt like getting off his chest everything he'd failed to at The Groucho. They could shake hands and say their farewells at the nearest services, and that would be that. His mind raced, but his body froze as he clutched the steering wheel.

"I appreciate this," said Tony. "I always appreciate a favour. I've done a lot of favours for people over the years. I did a lot of favours for you, didn't I?"

"You did," said Odilio automatically.

"I always speak highly of you. I tell everyone what a good lad you are. Got you a lot of work in the past, more than you realise, I think... It's nice to be able to return a favour."

Was this returning a favour? Odilio wondered. A lift home and a cup of coffee before calling a taxi? "Because a lot of people have decided to forget me," Tony continued. "I need people to stand up for me. I'm suing Sky for setting me up.

152

Those fucking cunts. I'm going to need people who can put a word in for my good character. I know I can count on you to have my back. It's not just what you promised the other night: it's the little things, like this, you know what I mean?"

"I know what you mean," said Odilio.

"Speaking of, our evening together made the papers. Did you see?"

"I did," Odilio turned briefly, studying Tony's face for the smallest sign of his betrayal.

"Can't get any privacy these days, can you?" Tony laughed. "They'll stick a long lens in the Groucho just to fill a few column inches." He chuckled again as Odilio's thoughts veered back to ideas of vacating Tony swiftly from the car.

23

Like the adjoining infinity pool, the giant lawn seemed to go on forever, or until, at

least, the cliff edge of the garden, where it dropped away and the sea began — a sea

of the most perfect and pure marine aqua-blue, carrying the horizon out to

somewhere beyond the little white sailboats, where it mingled with the cloudless

sky that was clear and silent save for the occasional squawk of seabirds. Away from

the sea, following the lawn up towards the brilliant white mansion that sparkled in

the afternoon sun, a team of staff were set to work, dressed in brilliant white outfits

that seemed to be cut from the same material as the house, and also the sailboats,

and also, the seabirds in the overhead sky. They unfolded the tables and set the

tablecloths in a practised manner while others started the barbecues, which were

really just giant outdoor gas stoves, and others, still, got to work setting out the

house silverware on tables, and putting down trays of cold food, covered for the

flies, and putting out drinks in ice-filled buckets, and glasses, and fruit.

  "I'd forgotten how gorgeous your place is," said Helena, topping up her

glass of white wine with soda water. She scanned the garden, where guests were

gathering in small groups. "You didn't have to do all this for us."

  "Oh, it's nothing, really," said Elizabeth, watching over her friend's

shoulder with an eye on her numerous staff. "We have these little get-togethers all

the time — it's quite normal." She looked around, checking for her husband and

then her guests, one by one. When she was satisfied everything was in order, she returned her attention to Helena with an intentness that sought to compensate for its momentary lapse. "It's so good to have you," said Elizabeth, rubbing her friend's arm. "So nice to get the chance to meet Elias — I hope he's enjoying himself."

"Oh, he's loving it," said Helena, whose turn it was now to scan the garden. A few metres away, talking to Julian and a politician Helena vaguely recognised from a scandal more than any political work, was Sylvie Dupont, fashion icon, luxury brand heiress and bullish art buyer: the bullseye of their target, a successful meeting with whom Helena's hopes for the weekend depended on. Helena returned her attention to Elizabeth. She knew such things must happen organically. Even so much as a stray glance returned could help forge a weakened opinion of her in the eyes of Madame Dupont.

"Ah!" Helena ejected. "In fact, here he is." At the edge of the party, in a gap between two barbecues, Elias appeared in his Burberry outfit the house staff had gone to great lengths to dry-clean. As soon as he saw Helena, he came over, clutching a bottle of champagne in one hand and a glass of it in the other. He approached them loosely with an uncharacteristic bounce to his step. "This is fucking brilliant," he announced, taking in the view of the garden. "Elizabeth, great to see you," he took her hand and kissed it. Helena glanced at her friend, who was reassessing the character that had been so shy in London.

"Lovely to see you, Elias," she replied in a playful tone.

"Wow, this weather is just so good. And your garden," Elias looked around like an enthusiastic child before topping himself up. "Anyone care for some?" he asked the women.

"We're good, thank you," Helena smiled politely.

"I can't believe it," Elias said, looking around again. "I mean, my mum's place is about the same size, but it's in fucking Sweden. *Sweden*. What's the point of being rich in Sweden? You can't have an infinity pool in Sweden. There's no point having your own BBQ unit when it's below zero half the year."

"I'm glad you like it," said Elizabeth.

"Do you have a yacht?"

"Just a little boat; Julian's the sailor," she nodded towards her husband, who was laughing loudly at one of the politician's jokes.

"We have to go out on it," Elias said seriously. "Hels, how about that? A boat ride, the three of us?"

"Now?" Helena chuckled. "I think the food is almost ready."

"Now, later; next week — I think I'm going to live here. Why don't we live here?" He looked at both of them, waiting for their reaction.

"I'm going to find my husband," Elizabeth said to Helena. "We can discuss your move later, Elias. I love your enthusiasm. I had the same reaction when Julian first brought me here. Give me a minute: I'll be back shortly."

"Be careful," Helena said, her eyes following the bottle. "I'd take a break from that if I were you: you don't want to make a fool of yourself." Elias' eyes wandered from her face down to her pastel-blue playsuit. How well it accentuated her round, perfect arse. And those white strappy heels on her tanned feet. Wasn't now the perfect moment? The fine weather, the picturesque lawn party: the pair of them on the cusp of some breakthrough in the art world, all the direct consequence

of the fruits of his unique imagination? They could sneak off for thirty minutes —
no one would have to know. Elias had almost forgotten about the line he'd done
before leaving his room, which was perhaps making him more direct in the present
occasion. Of course, there was no risk in sneaking a gram of the stuff onto a plane
— everyone does it — the only issue was that he'd soon require more.

"I need you to be relaxed. Let me do the talking. We don't want to give
away too much at this point or come across like we've got something to sell. We're
just lightly opening up a route to further communication. These things take a
while... Are you alright?"

"Kiss me," said Elias.

"I beg your pardon?"

He hadn't imagined her to look quite so shocked at the proposal. He tried
again. "Give me a kiss on my lips, now. Come on, I know you want it."

Helena flinched. "Don't be an idiot," she hissed.

Elias swallowed. "We can go somewhere more private?" The lump grew in
his throat like injector foam.

"What makes you think I'd want to do anything like that?" She examined
him for a second, her expression a mixture of anger and confusion. "Who do you
take me for?"

Elias tried to feign a relaxedness to the rebuke. "Chill out," he said,
pouring himself another large glass. He gulped it down quickly. "Uh-oh," he said,
smiling as he peered over her shoulder. "Look who's coming."

Elizabeth was making her way to the pair of them, her arm threaded into Sylvie's. Helena shot Elias an urgent look — a look pleading him to behave. "Madame Dupont," Helena exclaimed as the two neared. They exchanged kisses on each cheek, and Elias was invited to do the same.

"This is my lovely friend Helena who I've known forever," Elizabeth introduced her. "And this is Elias Karlsson, a very exciting London-based artist who you simply have to meet. Elias was just talking about moving here, actually."

"Not a bad idea," Sylvie remarked in her thick accent. She was in her mid to late sixties, with olive skin and dark hair. There was a scruffy, bohemian quality to the way she was dressed — a look common to the most esteemed billionaires. "And you're not the first one to have it, either," she glanced around. The others laughed, but Elias didn't. Elizabeth detected a shift had occurred in their conversation in the minutes she was gone.

"Anyway," said Elizabeth, "I've been meaning to ask Elias about the exhibition he's taking to Berlin next year. Hearts, is it? We actually bought one of his paintings the other week."

"Hearts," Sylvie repeated. "I like that name." The three women looked at Elias.

"Thanks," he said, bringing the champagne glass to his lips, pausing, then knocking it back in one.

"From what I can gather, it's all about bridging the distance between ourselves," said Helena, with a rare twang of nerves in her voice. "It's about opening up the world so it can become a place of love, rather than of hate and fear.

It's a collection that provides us with hope. There's a narrative within the pieces. We actually have the centrepiece in our house in London."

"Oh yes, you do!" Elizabeth interjected.

"A really gorgeous sculpture called 'Come and Get It'. Look, I have it on my phone." She scrolled through her photo album to show Sylvie. Sylvie strained to look. "It's so wonderful," said Helena. Sylvie took her glasses from her bag. She put them on and squinted at the phone.

"*Mais*, what's it to do with love?"

"Well," said Helena. "From my understanding, it's saying that women are the apex of love — that all love starts and ends with women, but I mean—"

"Doesn't he know?" Sylvie turned to Elias, who was watching them with a glossed-over expression.

"Of course," Helena swallowed. "Elias, why don't you explain?"

"Pffff," he said. "To be honest, Sylvie, I haven't a clue. I did it when I was younger and had to come up with some bullshit explanation to exhibit it all together. The galleries force you to do that. I mean, Hearts: it's as bullshit as it gets. It's 'love thy neighbour' for the trendies."

It was their first time hearing Sylvie Dupont laugh. "So, what are you working on now?" she asked. "If that stuff was for fun — why are you an artist?"

Elias shrugged. "I'm not an artist."

"Fair enough," her grin turned to shocked amusement as she looked at the others.

"Elias likes to be provocative," said Helena. "He's very shy about his work, that's all. He's doing some great things at the moment. What was that CCTV project you wanted to do in Hong Kong?"

Elias smiled at Helena, a naughty, destructive smile like a child who has soiled themselves on a trip and knows their parents must take responsibility for cleaning it up. "What Hong Kong project?" he replied.

"You know, the one you were telling me about last week. Chinese state surveillance?"

"Ah," said Elias. "My karate plan?"

Helena forced a loud laugh. "Stop it," she feigned a teasing tone.

Elias watched her coldly. He turned to Sylvie. "So basically, I'm trying to achieve the hardest one-inch punch possible. It can be a performance piece if you want it to be."

"Sorry," said Sylvie, confused. "Wuninch punch?" She looked to Elizabeth for clarification.

"One inch," Elias repeated. "Two and a half centimetres in metric. A two and a half centimetre punch, I guess they call it here." Sylvie Dupont looked as if she understood nothing. Elias punched the air as the three women flinched. "See? Bruce Lee could shatter a man's ribs with that punch. Speaking of, have you seen a snake skeleton? You have to see their ribs, man: they're crazy. Let me show you on my phone."

Julian called across the garden for Elizabeth: an executive decision was required over the meats. "I think my husband needs me," she apologised, exchanging a short pitying look to Helena. Helena glanced at Sylvie, who took the opportunity to leave as well. Sometimes a window of opportunity is no bigger than a letter box. Sylvie waved onwards, across the lawn, at someone she knew. "Lovely to meet you," she gushed, the words doppler shifted by the speed of her exit. Faced with Elias on her own, Helena said nothing. She took herself to the end of the garden, basking in the late afternoon sun that kissed the surface of the sea. She reached into her clutch bag to distract herself with her phone and texted her husband. *How is Scotland? Miss you.*

A minute later she received a reply: *Scotland great. Miss you too XX.*

24

Odilio put his phone back in his pocket and looked up just in time to witness Tony being sick into a privet bush. "Better out than in," said Tony. "Unless it's Halle Berry's cunt." Phillip watched, too, as three bursts of watery, shellfish-ridden vomit deposited into his garden. Tony belched and straightened his back when he was done. "Feel much better," he said. "Must have been a dodgy clam." Phillip handed Tony his handkerchief, who wiped his mouth and stuffed it into his pocket. "Feeling much better, actually," he repeated, taking in the front of the house as the three of them made their way across the gravel drive.

Tabitha was lying on the floor by the fireplace when her father entered. She was sorting through a pile of pinecones with Rachel. Some painted ones were drying on a sheet of newspaper. "Evening, everyone," Odilio ejected as he entered the room. "Hello, my darling Tabitha."

"Hello, Daddy," she said as he kissed her on the forehead. "We found loads of pinecones on our walk, and we're going to paint them *all*."

"A brilliant idea," said Odilio, picking up the largest one for his inspection.

"We're going to get some glitter for them when we're back in London, aren't we?" said Rachel.

"Yes," said Tabitha. "We're going to make Christmas pinecones."

There was a clattering in the hallway bathroom, then the door burst open, and Tony appeared, followed closely behind by Phillip. "You can keep that toothbrush," said Phillip, passing it back to him.

"I'm good," said Tony, wiping his mouth with his sleeve.

"Tabitha, do you remember Tony?" Odilio gestured to the door. "He's the man who gives you all that birthday money every year."

"Tabitha!" Tony shouted. He charged towards the fireplace.

"Tony!" she replied, matching the enthusiasm. "We're painting pinecones!"

"What a clever girl," he said, ruffling her hair, and browsing her handiwork.

"Do you want one? You can pick any one you like except this one."

Tony scanned the pile and reached for the one closest to him. "Thank you very much," he said, inspecting it briefly, and then placing it in his pocket.

Odilio cleared his throat. "Tony's had a bit of trouble with his house. We're going to look for a hotel for him to stay in, aren't we, Tony?"

"Why can't Tony stay here?" said Tabitha. "We have hundreds of rooms."

Odilio stared into the hearth, avoiding Tony's gaze. "Well, it's not our house, is it Tabs?"

Tabitha said nothing and continued with her painting.

"So who have we got here?" said Tony, scanning the faces of the others.

"This is Rachel, Tabitha's au pair," said Odilio.

"A pleasure to meet you."

163

"You too," she said.

"And that's Stuart," Odilio gestured to the armchair, where the tutor sat reading a book. He waved over.

"What wonderful people," said Tony. "What lovely people you have around you." He studied the face of the au pair. "Let's make a toast while I'm here. Odilio — fix us some drinks." Odilio glanced at Phillip, who pointed unenthusiastically to the spirit cabinet in the corner. "A scotch, my good man. And what's the young lady drinking?"

"Oh, I don't really drink," said Rachel.

"Don't *really*," Tony mimicked with feigned disgust. "Is that a 'you do' or 'you don't'?"

"Sometimes," she said.

"Then one scotch for the young lady so we can toast."

"Okay—"

"And you, sir?" Tony turned to the tutor.

Stuart shrugged and closed his book. "Scotch," he said.

"I count four," Tony nodded to Odilio. "I'm not going to be hard on Helena's brother here."

"Good," said Phillip. "Haven't touched a drop in three years."

"Any regrets?" Tony asked.

"None at all," Phillip said.

Odilio poured the drinks and handed them around. Tony passed one to the tutor and another to the au pair. "Gather round," he instructed. He pulled a stool up to the fireplace and squatted down. "A toast to the highland life," he said, as their four glasses touched. "To good health and great company; to loyalty and loyal friends. May God protect us all."

Stuart perched on the floor beside the fire. The poacher's priest had been cleaned and left to dry. The tutor picked it up, oblivious to its purpose. He fancied it was made from yew wood. He rolled it across the palm of his hand, thinking it looked like a police truncheon, then put it back where he'd found it. "I was chatting to your gamekeeper this afternoon, Phillip," said Stuart. "I hear tomorrow's the big day."

"Father Tom?" Odilio interrupted. "He's still here, right?"

"He is," said Phillip. "That's him."

"He was fantastic the last few times I visited."

"He's a legend," Phillip said, proudly. "A brilliant beater and an even better stalker."

"He told me you were hunting red stags tomorrow," said Stuart.

"Eh, yes," said Phillip. He looked cautiously at the tutor. "I think that's right."

"Red stags tomorrow?" said Tony, his ears pricking up. "You're hunting? Why didn't you say so?" He nudged Odilio.

"I must have forgotten," Odilio shrugged in reply.

"Odilio must have mentioned I have one of the best stalkers in Scotland. Leroy Jones: you'll know him if you ever read those hunting magazines. Now, he's a *real* highland boy."

"What's the weather like tomorrow?" Stuart asked.

"It's meant to be a clear one," said Tony.

"I heard that, too," said Rachel. "It's going to be a nice, sunny day."

"That's what we want to hear, isn't it?" Tony was smiling.

"It was meant to be Tabitha's first stalk," said Odilio, the defeat audible in his voice.

Tony licked his lips. The light was back in his eyes. "Tabitha, don't you want to shoot deer with a real Scot who's wrestled bears, fought wolves, and tickled hippopotamuses?"

Tabitha laughed. She always found Tony amusing. There was something theatrical about him: something children could appreciate. He was like a real-life clown. "I don't want to shoot," she said, placing a pinecone on her pile.

"*Tony*," said Odilio. "We're not just shooting. There's more to it than that."

"There's everything more to it than that," Tony chuckled, resting a meaty hand on the brickwork of the fireplace. "What about you?" he turned to Rachel. "Are you coming?"

"No way," said Rachel. "I'd be useless. I've never even seen a gun."

"Never seen a gun!" Tony shook his head. "We could get you started on a Remington. A smart .223. Hardly any recoil; good for a girl. A beautiful gun that packs a punch."

"I don't want to shoot anything," she said. "I wouldn't be much fun."

"Suit yourself. Maybe you could come and watch?"

166

"Let's get looking for that hotel," said Odilio, putting down his glass.

"And you, boy?" Tony ignored him. "Ever nabbed a stag?"

Stuart shrugged. "Never killed anything bigger than a wasp."

"Afraid to do the job yourself? No qualms buying meat from the supermarket?"

"No, actually, I don't eat meat at all."

Tony smiled at Odilio. "You've brought a vegetarian to a hunting estate?" He burst out laughing. "That's very clever."

"He's Tabitha's tutor, and he's not coming," said Odilio.

Tony studied the young man. "Why the hell not? He should do. Then he can have an opinion on the whole business. Don't you agree?" He jabbed a finger in the tutor's direction.

"I guess we won't have a tutorial tomorrow if Tabitha's out with you," Stuart said.

"Exactly!" Tony roared. "See, he wants to come! And who can blame him for wanting to be part of the action? He can join me in the Hummer with Leroy. That man will give you an education." Tony was almost skipping with enthusiasm. "And you, young lady: you'd be more than welcome to have a seat in the back with me...."

"I really would prefer to stay here," Rachel said.

"We should sort that hotel," said Odilio.

Tony stood up. "Okay, okay, I know when I'm not wanted."

"It's just we need to get dinner sorted for Tabs...."

Tony swatted him away. "What time are we thinking tomorrow? I'll have Leroy prepare the guns."

"First light, I guess," said Odilio. "7ish."

"7 o'clock: I'll be here." He put on his coat.

Odilio thought about interrupting, protesting, making his excuses, but the nuisance was leaving; he did not want to stall things now. "Will you take the hotel in Aviemore?" Phillip asked.

"No need, my man. Now I have every reason to knock on Leroy's door. He can put me up for the night." Odilio knew Tony was still over the limit, but the issue seemed less important now. The old meathead took his keys from his pocket. "I should be alright," he said, aware of what the others were thinking. "Sobered up on that drive. Any longer here, and I'll fall asleep."

"Good to see you, Tony," said Odilio.

"And I'll see you all tomorrow. Thanks for a lovely lunch, gentlemen."

25

"Of course, you don't have to come tomorrow," Odilio said, cutting the lamb meat into cubes on the kitchen counter. "There's no pressure. Tony can be like that sometimes — rather forceful. It's entirely up to you."

Stuart was mincing garlic for a salad dressing. He stopped what he was doing and turned to Odilio. "I've read about him in the news lately," he said in a low voice. "He seems to have a precedent of getting what he wants. I could see that this afternoon."

"Interesting," Odilio replied. Strangely, he hadn't considered that the others might know about Tony. He'd been so invested in his online reputation, he hadn't stopped to consider that those in his locality were people, too, privy to the same information. The remark reminded him to tell Helena that Tony was in Scotland: she would find out herself soon enough. But tell her he was coming on the hunt? There was no way of explaining that — he could hardly justify it to himself.

"It's true," said Odilio. "He's always been somewhat of a bully."

"Why did you invite him?" Stuart asked. Discomfort with the tutor's directness gave way to contemplation over an answer. Odilio placed the chopped meat into the mixing bowl and massaged in the marinade. He would text Helena as soon as he was done.

"He invited himself," said Odilio. "Can't you see, I don't want him here? If anything, I've been trying to get away from him."

"Right," said the tutor. Odilio paused, taking in the insufficiency of his remark. "In fact, tomorrow might be the last time I ever see him. It's just a feeling, mind. You don't have to come, but I'd appreciate some sensitivity in the meantime." He nodded to the chopping board for them to continue without the questions.

They finished their dishes in silence. Once the lamb had undergone a quick marinade, Odilio put the pieces onto skewers, as the tutor whisked together a vinaigrette that he added to the bowl of sliced tomatoes and avocado.

"You know, I'm quite interested, actually," said Stuart, after a few minutes.

"In Tony?" Odilio replied.

"To come tomorrow. I'm not sure I told you, but I lived in Spain for a few years. Back then, I used to hang out with a lot of what you'd call 'hippies'. We used to block lorries full of livestock from entering the abattoirs. Occasionally, the drivers would let one of the animals go. A chicken or a sheep or something — in good faith, and to get rid of us. It was important for me to see the bits of the industry they wanted to hide. Have you ever been to an abattoir?"

"I haven't," said Odilio. "Can't say I ever wanted to, to be honest."

"Well, you couldn't even if you did," said Stuart. "They're some of the most off-limit spaces in the world. They don't let anyone in apart from the workers and, believe me, they vet those more thoroughly than the Secret Service. They can't have anyone expose them, ever. If you took one look inside a slaughterhouse, you'd never buy any of those products again."

170

"So you've been inside?"

The tutor shook his head. "I haven't. But a friend broke into one and was run over by a forklift truck."

"Was he killed?"

"No, but her legs were crushed."

"That's very sad," said Odilio, tasting the dressing again. He took a piece of cling film from the drawer and covered the bowl with it.

"I've seen enough of that to make me wary of the whole thing. I mean, you only run someone over if you're in the wrong, right?"

"I guess so. It was on purpose then?"

"They had to pull the driver off, he wanted to keep going with his fists."

A member of the kitchen staff entered the kitchen. "Grill ready, sir," he told Odilio, who handed him the tray of kebabs. The chef looked at them, then at Odilio. "The boss dinnae like things tae spicy."

"I'm sure Phillip can handle a bit of paprika," Odilio snorted. "How long will they take?"

"Should be fifteen minutes."

"Good," said Odilio. "I'm going to get changed."

In the hallway, Odilio ran into Rachel who was coming down the stairs. "Hey," she stopped him at the bottom of the staircase.

"Everything alright?" Odilio replied. "Dinner is in fifteen minutes."

"Everything is great," she replied. "It's just… I've been thinking about tomorrow."

171

"I've already discussed it with Stuart. He invited himself, there's nothing I can do…"

"I'm talking about Tabitha."

"Okay?" He raised an eyebrow. "What about her?"

"Don't you think she's a bit young? I don't know. I'm worried it's going to be quite intense, and she's only nine… Maybe I'm overthinking."

"I think you are," Odilio smiled. "She's tough for a nine-year-old. She was great at fishing. We're going to take it gently. You're more than welcome to join and see for yourself."

"I'm really okay," said Rachel. "But thank you. It's just your friend, what's his name again?"

"Tony?" Odilio wondered if she'd read the news, too.
"Yeah. He just seems to be quite serious about it. In a good way, I mean. But she's just a beginner. Maybe it's a bad mix."

"I get your point," said Odilio. "I'll have a think. But we're quite happy taking the risk. I think Helena's as keen as I am."

"Okay," said Rachel. "Well, sorry to bother you, anyway."

In the guest bedroom, Odilio switched into his tracksuit bottoms and a t-shirt. Perched on the end of his bed, he deliberated again over sending the text to Helena. A sense of connection between his thoughts and words was slowly but surely emerging. Tomorrow would be the last day he'd see Tony. He'd said it and meant it. The rumblings of action were taking hold in his soul: the rising desire to put it clearly to his old friend threatened to become material. Patience was key in

172

these situations. He would not tell Helena tonight, but tomorrow, when things had come to a conclusion. He knew the extent of his wife's contempt for that man — recent events only confirmed what she'd long held to be true. Indeed, Odilio suspected there was more he didn't know. Tony had an outrageous self-belief in his charms: a fantasy that had swollen in size the more discrepant from reality it had become. When Tony asked about Helena, it was like he was checking in on an old flame. Helena had never mentioned anything, but Odilio suspected Tony of having tried it on with her in the past. Of course, his wife would never have taken up the offer, but he knew his old friend's twisted imagination: in rejection, Tony could hallucinate lust, regret, and the promise of an imminent U-turn. Tony thought about one thing in the company of Helena. Anyone with the most basic training in psychology could see it in his eyes. They were eyes from which it looked like tentacles might extend.

Odilio pulled out his phone and returned to the Daily Mail article. He'd avoided checking who was sharing it on Twitter — he'd avoided Twitter as much as he could since arriving in Scotland. He scrolled through the photographs of the two of them. What could anyone seeing those images think beyond the obvious? It looked like what it looked like: two friends colluding in a private rebuke of myriad sexual harassment allegations. What nuance did he suppose shone through that could convince anyone he was not on the wrong side here? He supposed the photos were taken late into the night. His cherry-red cheeks and idiot grin testified to his being in the latter stages of inebriation. How had the plan gone so badly? He'd meant to draw a line under their friendship, not solidify it in the public eye like

173

some vow renewal in the announcements section of a local newspaper. He could not afford to make the same mistake tomorrow.

Why was it so hard to put his foot down? he wondered, rubbing his temples. Odilio was a no-nonsense restaurant critic. Someone who called a spade a spade, and a substandard, over-priced plate of Haute cuisine, just that. In the reality of his daily life, however, he was incapable of such directness. Of course, it was no accident Tony was a difficult man to say no to. His coercive tendencies explained his astronomical rise in the industry. His bullying behaviour had got him this far: an exaggerated machismo that repelled women and cowed men under a veneer of fraternal loyalty. Tony had been enabled by cowardice. The crumbs he threw back gave the illusion he was returning the favour. Odilio lay on the bed, staring up at the ceiling. Everything was going to be fine, he told himself. The intercom system buzzed and broke the reverie. Dinner was served in the dining room.

26

The house was silent. Philip had taken himself off to bed after dinner, complaining of a bad stomach. The staff had returned to their quarters in the eastern wing. In the guest room, Odilio was making a start on his Blue Langoustine piece. His method, when it came to writing a restaurant review, was to jot down his observations in a stream of consciousness journal: then, from the slurry, pick out the gems, using those to inform the main structure of the article (it was his primary business to entertain; the folly of the aspiring food writer was to insist on being comprehensive). Tonight, nothing was forthcoming. His editor's words nagged at him as he sat at the desk. *I need everyone to pull something special out of the bag.* Odilio knew he had to come up with the goods. But he was struggling to remember even the most basic details of the lunch. A bad feeling tainted his memory, which seemed unable to manifest anything concrete — much less anything related to the food. He was tired and ready for bed. The dinner sat heavily in his stomach. He belched; the scent of spices came back to him. It felt like a layer of kebab grease was coating the inside of his gullet.

Within minutes, he'd given up. Odilio put down his notepad and switched off the desk light. He dressed in his pyjamas and unmade the bed. Before climbing in, he checked the corridor, thinking he'd heard a noise. Tabitha's light was on. He knocked on her door — a sleepy voice told him he could enter — he pushed it gently open. Tabitha was lying in bed, looking across the room at the silhouette in

175

the doorway. She sat up and rubbed her eyes. The bedroom smelled of mildew and old books. A drab, 1950s-style wallpaper decorated the walls. "Everything okay, Tabs?" said Odilio, edging forward. "Why's the light on?" He sat at the end of the bed. The frame creaked under his weight.

"I can't sleep," she said. On the bedside table, Odilio noticed an opened copy of a Beatrix Potter book.

"Would you like me to read it to you?" Odilio said, glancing at it.

"No, thanks," said Tabitha. "It's really boring."

"Oh," said Odilio. "Fair enough." He squeezed her foot through the blanket. "Why can't you sleep?" Tabitha rested her chin in her hands. "Is Tabitha sad? I could have a look in the library if you want me to? See if there's something a bit more interesting? Maybe an adventure book or a murder mystery?"

"I don't want to shoot the deer," Tabitha blurted out.

"My baby," Odilio said. "Why didn't you say so earlier? No one is forcing you to shoot anything. We're not here to do things you don't want to do."

Tabitha rubbed her nose and sniffed. "Tony said we're shooting deers. I like deers; I don't want to shoot one."

Odilio laughed. "Tony says lots of silly things. If we believed everything he said, we'd be in the loony bin. We love Tony, but the man tells more stories than Beatrix Potter!" He reached over to tap the cover with his knuckles.

"So why are we going tomorrow?"

He sighed and twisted on the bed-end to face her directly. "Let's put it this way," he said. "Do you like burgers?"

176

Tabitha nodded.

"Where do burgers come from?"

"Cows," she said.

"Precisely. And cows have to die to make delicious burgers. Do you understand?"

"Yes."

"Well, that's how it works: how it's always worked, see. Eating meat is in our nature. Every society since the dawn of time has eaten it and always will. There's no way back from that. Meat is delicious — it makes us happy — but most importantly, we need it to stay healthy. That's why we're here." He paused for a moment, letting the silence linger as his words sunk in.

"Tabs, I believe it's important for someone who eats meat to at some point in their life see how the process is done. I don't think it's right to expect someone else to do all the dirty work. Why should I enjoy the burger but have no role in making it? It's in our nature to eat meat, but it's also in our nature to hunt the meat in the first place. That's what's missing these days. Everything is done for us: we enjoy all the rewards without putting in any effort. It's like having pudding for every meal — it might be fun for a while, but soon it's going to make you sick, fat, and spotty." Odilio pinched Tabitha's nose.

"I want pudding for every meal," she giggled.

"That's why I want to take you hunting, so you can see how it's done. Then you can judge for yourself. You can say you never want to do it again, but at least this way you tried."

"But," Tabitha said, stroking her chin. "Stuart said we aren't supposed to eat animals, and if we were, we'd have big claws and sharp teeth like lions."

"Then add Stuart to the list of people who talk nonsense!" Odilio's eyes widened. "See, Stuart is a smart person. A very smart person. But he's a vegetarian! He doesn't eat meat. He's never gone hunting. How can he know anything if he hasn't tried it? I used to think like that at his age. But sharp teeth? Claws? Tabitha — we have guns! Guns are our teeth and claws. These are what our big brains produced. They're ours, aren't they? Lions don't have guns last time I checked. Tigers don't have bows and arrows. Just because these things aren't stuck to us doesn't mean they aren't *part of us*."

Odilio fancied his words were getting through to her. He repositioned himself on the bed, resting his back against the frame. "Let me share something else with you," he said. "Years ago, my father — your grandfather — took me hunting here in Scotland. I was younger than you are and even more nervous. We went out one morning, just as we can do tomorrow, to hunt a red stag. Now, I didn't want to. I wondered, what was the point? Why not just get some burgers from the supermarket and save ourselves the hassle of waking up at five in the morning, in the pouring rain, walking for miles. But my father explained to me something on the way there that has stuck with me ever since. He said that just a few thousand years ago, Britain wasn't an island. It was connected to the whole of Europe by a strip of land that's now entirely under the sea. All the red stags in Britain were just the same red stags from the continent, and all of them were hunted by wolves. There are no wolves in Britain, now. Humans drove them out. Nothing hunts the red stag

178

anymore. A good thing, you might imagine, but no, not at all. Red stags are beset with problems because of this. For one, their population is too big. There are too many of them, and not enough food for them all to eat. The weakest starve; the children are always hungry. The stags resort to foraging food in areas they wouldn't usually go, in order to meet their extra needs. They destroy other habitats in the process. Disease and malnutrition are rife. You see, when they were hunted by wolves — when they were connected to their European cousins — they were actually happier. There was enough food; they didn't need to put themselves in danger. The red stag's lives were more fulfilling. Other animals flourished, too, because the stags weren't trampling their houses. Nature is a balance. Now, *we* hunt the stags to maintain that balance — to ensure everything keeps working properly. I understood immediately what my father meant. I remember that first trip like it was yesterday. It was freezing. I couldn't feel my cheeks or fingertips. We must have walked ten miles. Dad said: 'We'll come back with a stag, or we won't come back at all'. I believed him. And so it was an incredible sight to walk into a clearing filled with deer after several hours in pursuit. He let me set up the rifle; he took the shot and made it first go. Dad butchered the stag that evening and put the meat in the freezer. It lasted a year: this one animal, which had to be killed in the first place. It must have fed hundreds. Much better, you accept, than going to the shops for burgers."

Tabitha was focused on the words of her father. Only the slightest furrowing of her brow conveyed any final misgivings. "So we're the wolves now?" she asked.

"In a way, we are," said Odilio. "But wolves aren't so bad, you see. Certainly not as bad as the stories make them out to be. Nature needs wolves."

"Then why did we get rid of them?"

"Good question." Odilio scratched his cheek. "Man playing god, I guess. He sees the wolf and thinks there can't be any good reason for that creature and that he'd be better off getting rid of it. Well, more fool man." Odilio sat up. "Anyway, I hope this chat might help you rethink tomorrow. I don't want to force you, but I think you'll be missing out on something really important if you don't come. Even Stuart is joining. We're never too old to learn."

Tabitha pulled the blanket up to her neck. She slid further down into the bed.

"Actually, can you read me that story, please?" she asked.

Odilio beamed and took the book from the bedside table. "Of course I can," he said in a triumphant voice.

27

Helena was standing at what had become a familiar spot over the course of the
weekend. The patioed tip of the Walkers' estate, beyond the infinity pool and
bamboo bar, on the last bit of slabbed land before the precipice of this rocky
promontory, was the only place in the villa where she could get a good phone
signal. Helena was trying to reach Elias, upon whom she craved to unleash the pent
up fury the weekend had fomented. The call went through to voicemail. At the same
time, she did her best to carry herself with a light-heartedness that would dispel any
notions in others that something had gone wrong. A feigned, perfectly believable
casualness with the situation that said: "These things happen all the time", and
"that's just Elias!". Inside, Helena was seething like a pressure cooker. She took a
cigarette from her handbag and put it to her lips. She indulged occasionally —
indulged more on the continent than at home — and indulged heavily when
stressed. The stars were aligned. She smoked the cigarette quickly while a young
pool boy in a white polo shirt dredged leaves nearby from the water with a net.

Elias had disappeared. After the meeting with Sylvie had collapsed into a
demonstration of short-distance punching, he was nowhere to be found. In his
absence, Helena had done her best to patch up the lacklustre impression he'd made,
but there was no saving the unsalvageable. Sylvie didn't deal with 'loose cannons'
or artistic 'mavericks'. She was a sensible, business-driven art buyer and as such
every instinct of hers repelled her from Elias and Helena by association. No love

lost. Sylvie Dupont had left the garden party a short while afterwards. The moment was gone. It marked the sort of professional failure hitherto unheard of in Helena's career. One she was still struggling to make sense of.

Meanwhile, Elias had asked a driver to take him to Nice, to a bar in town. His phone had been switched off all evening. But Helena wouldn't so easily forget. The events of the afternoon were replaying in her mind. What had Elias been playing at, trying to kiss her like that? Ruining the weekend in retaliation for rejection. Helena had already decided her next move. She had drafted the message with her lawyer and would send a copy of it to the Karlsson family in the morning. It was over. She would drop him. Of course, her investors had made substantial commitments to the Karlsson brand; it was going to cost her reputation. She could work on the cosmetics of their separation later. Right now it was costing her even more to go down the rabbit hole with him, into whatever abyss awaited him there.

It was nighttime. Helena paced the patio, trying his phone again. No luck. She stubbed out the cigarette and took a deep breath. Tomorrow she'd fly home without him. She would get to her brother's place and think things through there. Elizabeth appeared at the patio door with two glasses of wine. "Thought you could use a drink," she smiled. They sat at one of the tables facing the sea. "Tough day," she added.

"For me or for you?"

"Both of us," Elizabeth laughed. "God, it's no fun hosting. I think this is the first moment of the day I've been able to relax and it's past midnight."

"It was a great afternoon," Helena said.

"Thank you. I hope you managed to enjoy yourself in the end. I'm sorry things didn't pan out with Sylvie. Have you managed to get in touch with Elias yet?"

"Not yet," Helena said, stiffly.

"Well, I'm sure he's just letting off some steam."

*

Elias rolled up the twenty-euro bill and snorted the line off the table with an air of good practice. He sniffed a few times to stop any loose powder from vacating his nostrils, then took a shot of vodka to chase. A flailing hand lurched for the note, as someone took their turn to snort a line from the several that were cut on the table. A tingle of excitement preceded the familiar sensations of the drug: the strange feeling of his teeth, which wasn't exactly numbness (when do you ever feel your teeth?); the cold sweat that varnished his palms. "The girls here are crazy," Elias said, looking past the group at the table and into the sordid darkness of the club, from which only the bare flesh of the strippers, lit up by the sparse pink spotlights, seemed to create any recognisable forms. No one heard the remark; the music was too loud. Someone shouted: "Goose!" and everyone around him cheered. It was just that sort of place, he thought, joining in with the shouting. Everyone doing dumb shit, having a good time.

Goose. Elias chuckled to himself. He mouthed the word again. A sour drip was working its way down the back of his throat. He took another vodka shot from the table. "The girls here are crazy," he repeated as he eyed up a young woman in a g-string, holding a bottle of vodka, which she put down on the table, replacing it for

183

the finished one in the ice bucket. *Grey Goose*. He read the label and started laughing, running his tongue along his teeth, scanning the table and beholding his newly-made friends with a glow of self-satisfaction. He was good at meeting people. Wherever he went, he managed to get a crowd around him. The trick was simple: find the drugs. They made you the prized asset of any group looking for a good time. Elias was the man. Elias Karlsson. He didn't need the validation of some prissy old woman and her friends to know it. Yes, he was a living rebuke to his doubts: he was living that rebuke this very moment. A party of shit-hot influencers gathered around him like suckling pigs on his bountiful good-time teets. Elias Karlsson was the man.

"Hey, bro. After this we're going to a boat party," someone shouted in his ear, cutting off his meditation. Elias turned slowly to apprehend the figure sitting next to him. He was a young guy, barely in his twenties, with a mop of blonde hair and an irritating, round American face. "We're gonna go get fucked up on the boat."

Elias nodded. "The girls in here are crazy, man," he replied before returning his attention to the girl in the g-string, gesturing at her to come over for a dance.

28

The immaculate, white Hummer pulled into the Glendales' drive at seven in the morning. The horn bibbed several times, alerting the estate to its presence outside. Under the porch of the old stable, to the side of the main building, where the family stored the outdoor equipment: quad bikes, fishing tackle, rifles, and the like, Tom — Father Tom as he was affectionately referred to by those who knew him, or sometimes just 'The Father' because the winning theory was he looked like he'd recently escaped life in the clergy — was preparing the equipment for the day's hunt. The claxon ring of the horn had caused him to jump and almost packed in his seventy-six-year-old heart on the spot. He marched out onto the drive, recognising at once who was at the wheel of the vehicle (a stalker with a veritable reputation of his own). He assumed the portly gentleman in the passenger's seat was his client and remembered the boss had mentioned another party would be joining them. He raised his arm to signal to the driver he had seen them, then made his way up the drive, to the house, to tell the family their guests had arrived.

It had been years since Odilio last shared the company of Phillip's gamekeeper. Back when he visited the Glendales more often, he had grown fond of the Father, enjoying what he could only describe as his 'realness' — that is, his devotion to country pursuits and everything the life entailed. Father Tom was a man who lived and breathed the highlands. He belonged to the land, quite literally: he'd come with the estate's purchase and lived in a little cottage in the grounds, on the other side of a copse that backed onto the garden. It made his nickname more fitting, Odilio thought. The life of the country gentleman bore certain similarities to the clergy in its quiet, meditative devotion to the divine. "Good morning, Father," said Odilio, from the steps of the Glendales, looking up from the wellington boots he was struggling to get on his feet.

"Mornin', mornin', everyone," Father Tom called out cheerfully as he whipped around the yard, ensuring everything was in place for the hunt to go as smoothly as possible.

One by one, the hunting party stepped out of the house, into the radiant morning. A passing observer would have been struck by certain differences in the party's styles. Phillip, head to toe in the deer-stalking attire of the tradition, had undertaken painstaking research to ensure every piece of his outfit, down to the handkerchief in his pocket, was as authentic as it could be. Layered in the fashions of the golden era of sport shooting, he carried himself with new majesty, a lightness of footing; his usual stoop was no more. Instead, he stretched out long and proud in the gentle air, like a spring flower. To the passing observer, watching from a distance, Odilio would have appeared quite the same. In a tweed three-piece, wearing the same deer-stalking hat as his brother-in-law, it would only be on closer inspection that one would notice the elements borrowed from the 21st century. Gore-tex gaiters and brand-spanking wellington boots; high-performance Nikon binoculars, and a GPS optimizable compass made promises the 19th-century was unable to keep. But it was Tabitha whose outfit departed most strikingly from the colonial cosplay of the men. Dressed in a garish Disney anorak and sparkly pink

186

wellingtons, she had ignored her father's implied warnings that on the glen she would present an eye-sore. Stuart followed last, dressed in the get-up of the typical daytripper. A plastic waterproof onesie clung to his chain-store clothing, with his boots still caked in the remnants of last year's walking. He had taken heed of Odilio's advice that if the stalk went well it would involve a lot of laying down in damp grass — and if it went badly it would become what was known as "walking with stick", still a valuable lesson in the ways of the glen.

Father Tom was not so much as dressed up in anything. His Barbour coat and tweed shooting trousers looked as natural on him as skin. They were clothes that had been cared for and repaired at the very first signs of damage. They had been nurtured with love and knew his body as well as any physical part of him.

A flurry of horn sounds emitted from the Hummer as the family appeared on the drive. Tony leapt out of the passenger seat and roared his greetings. Dressed in a frayed pair of tracksuit bottoms, a space-age pair of Timberland boots, and a cream Aran jumper with a blue sports gilet, there was a crass, North American quality to him, Odilio thought. An image bolstered, no doubt, by the flashy, oversized vehicle he'd arrived in. At the same time, Father Tom reversed Phillip's vehicle out of the barn. A solid piece of military history growled as it pulled up in front of the house. Tony grinned at the sight of the battered jeep. His vehicle looked like the younger version of it on steroids. It was obnoxiously big, Odilio thought. Not that he cared for cars, but it was almost a psychological fact you purchased such a vehicle to compensate for something.

"Keys, sir," Father Tom called to Phillip through the window of the jeep. Phillip handed the Father a set of keys from his breast pocket. They were the keys to the gun cabinet. The guns were the last items to be loaded into the car, and they were always procured — despite having been cleaned and readied by the Father earlier that morning — with the final permission of the keeper of the house.

Small talk ensued between the party. Breaths formed wisps of vapour in the fresh air. Tabitha was stunned silent by the early wake-up, as well as the punishing frost of the morning. This was a cold that never found its way down to London. She looked at the landscape in a sort of daze while the others chatted.

Tony introduced his gamekeeper. "This is Leroy Jones," he gripped the man beside him on the shoulder. "An animal is this man. We've seen some things together over the years. Wouldn't trust anyone with my life as much as Leroy here." Odilio studied the gamekeeper. He was a short, wiry man in his early forties, whose default expression was a smirk and who avoided eye contact to the point of provocation. The gamekeeper scanned the grounds as if he were putting together a quote for a building job.

"Leroy was my beater in South Africa," said Tony. "Never trust a hunter in Africa; they'll rip you off for everything you've got. Drive you in circles for hours to shoot mongoose, then charge ten grand for the pleasure. All those reservation fees and bullshit. Luckily, I had Leroy with me. He knew what they were up to. He told them straight he was onto their scam. We rented our own vehicles. Paid off some park guards — they were boys, really — and went in there like Platoon. Took a Cape Buffalo, didn't we?"

188

"Took a few," Leroy said.

"We were in extinction mode," Tony laughed.

"I've never hunted outside of Scotland," said Phillip. "Somehow, it makes less sense to me, elsewhere. I can't, for instance, imagine hunting from a car."

"It's different in Africa," said Tony, blankly. "There are proper animals there. It's kill or be killed. A nasty place; you take every advantage you can."

"I spent many summers in Africa," said Phillip. "Lagos and Jo'burg. I don't doubt the stakes are higher — it's that I don't feel the same joy in the sport there. Here, we have tradition. It's the other fixtures that make deer stalking so unique. I blame the Yanks."

Tony grinned. "Well, speaking of, let me show you what we're packing today." He turned and reached through the window of the Hummer and took out his rifle, which he had stored on the backseat. It was a large, matte black semi-automatic. "The Mossberg 400, custom-built with a .308 calibre. It's an absolute weapon," he bashed the side of it proudly. "If you're lucky, I might let you have a go."

Father Tom loaded the rifles into the Jeep, stowing them in a cabinet in the back of the vehicle. "Let's be off," said Phillip, cupping his hands together. "The stags will be moving down the valley for the rut. The earlier we can get there, the better our chances. We're twenty minutes away from our docking point, then we have a good walk ahead of us."

Odilio, Phillip, and Tabitha joined Father Tom in the jeep. The tutor, for considerations of space, joined Tony and Leroy in the Hummer. "Good luck to him," said Odilio. They pulled out of the drive onto a track that led to the back of the house, directly through the grounds of the estate. The Hummer followed. "Do you know that gamekeeper?" Phillip asked the Father. "I'm sorry, but I don't trust him one bit."

"Leroy's not a bad boy," Father Tom grunted as he shifted the gear stick. Phillip knew it was a fundamental rule of a good gamekeeper never to talk badly about someone behind their back. A reputation could be quickly spoilt if you were heard talking rot about a colleague, or worse, a client. In such close-knit circles, you couldn't afford to make enemies. "I knew the boy's father well, truth be told. We used to fish trout together in Morlich."

"I don't trust him: his eyes are too close together," Phillip sniffed. "I don't trust Tony, either," he said, glancing at Odilio in the mirror. "Wouldn't trust him as far as I could throw him."

"What happened to his father?" asked Odilio.

Father Tom smacked his lips together and thought before answering. "Well, he went mad, he did. The family was sheep farmers back then. Lost half a flock one winter to the blight. Alastair gassed himself in his car. That was a sad winter."

The jeep bobbed up and down in the ruts of the dirt track. Soon, the road petered out into grassland, the route signalled only by the occasional pile of rocks. The flat moorland led to a hill range visible in the distance. Tabitha watched through the window as the scenery unfolded. "We're parking at the foot of the hill here," Odilio said, pointing to the distance. "We'll make our way up very carefully, then at the top, we'll have the most incredible view of the valley. Are you excited?"

"I'm very excited," said Tabitha.

"Me too," said Odilio, a slight nervousness building in him.

"If there are deer at the bottom, we're in luck," said Phillip from the front seat. "Back by lunchtime, I suspect. Back by dinner, if not." At that moment, the white Hummer pulled up by their side. Tony's top half protruded from the sun window. He was holding his rifle and swigging from a hip flask. They watched Tony take aim with his rifle at the horizon, slowly rotating around until it pointed at their car. He let out a triumphant laugh before dropping it back through the sun window and taking another drink. "Don't mind me, ladies!" The Hummer pulled ahead. "Vamos! Let's go, go, go!"

"Idiot," Phillip tutted.

"Tony is silly, isn't he?" Odilio said, squeezing Tabitha's hand. "Not like our Tom here. Tom, tell Tabitha how sensible you are."

"Aye, I can't tell a lie — especially not to a young lady."

Odilio laughed. "There we go: sensible as I said."

The jeep rocked over a mound of earth. Odilio held the handle of the roof to steady himself. "Now, Tabitha, one thing I wanted to tell you today, is that we're not here to kill a healthy deer, or a mother, or any creature that has a life left in it. We're only here to hunt the sick and the old. A deer with nothing to live for, isn't that right Uncle Phillip?"

"Exactly," said Phillip.

"Tom's done this since he was a little boy. He knows what to look out for. We listen to everything he says because he knows everything there is to know. Tom will tell us what deers we can take and what ones we can't. We respect that decision. His word is final."

"So we only kill grannies?" said Tabitha.

"Yes," said Odilio. "Grannies or grandads. Only if they're losing it, though." He looked ahead. "Sometimes it's more humane to kill something that's suffering than to let it continue to suffer, right?" Odilio squeezed Tabitha's hand again.

"Will you shoot a deer?" she asked.

"Maybe," he said. "But maybe there's nothing I need to kill. Maybe all the deer here are happy."

"Another thing you must know, Tabitha," said Phillip. "Is that the worst thing we can do is injure a deer and not kill it. That would only double its suffering and, of course, means we have nothing to eat. So we shoot them here," he gestured to his diaphragm. "We shoot them broadside — that means sideways. We lie down for the shot to ensure we're as accurate as can be. We follow a line up its leg, then continue until halfway up the body. That's when we pull the trigger. There's no way a deer survives the shot, especially not the old ones we're going for. It'll take a pace or two forwards, then that's that. We've freed it from its misery."

They parked at the foot of the hill. From here, they would walk to the neighbouring valley, where the wildest parts of the Glendales began and where they would most likely find deer. The sun beamed now over the moorland, illuminating

192

the rising moisture in a haze. Tony greeted them again as they stepped out of the jeep. He was as enthusiastic as if they'd been separated for weeks: jocular and in the early stages of inebriation. "What a gorgeous morning," he bellowed, stuffing his gilet pockets with gun shells and taking another long swig from the flask.

The Father distributed the guns from the jeep boot. In clusters, the hunting party began walking the trail that led over the hill into the next valley. Odilio found himself beside the tutor as they made the ascent. Stuart, who was not shooting, looked melancholic. "Everything OK?" Odilio asked. "Having doubts?" Ahead, Tony was attacking a thistle bush with his walking stick.

"I am William Wallace!" he shouted.

"Bit of a handful, isn't he?" said Odilio. "You drew the short straw in the car."

"He's a bit much," said the tutor. "He's making me uncomfortable with that gun."

It was a steep walk to the top, and the grass thinned as they gained height, making the earth slippery underfoot. Father Tom led the group, bounding with a naturalness that was easy on the eye. Strength in those legs forged from years of doing just this. Tendons like steel cables, the stick was merely decorative. The Father was followed closely behind by Tony and Leroy, both of whom were at pains to be at the front of the action. Phillip and the tutor walked together now, nattering over an affinity for the local birdlife. Odilio was left at the back with Tabitha. He held her hand, helping her navigate the peatier stretches of terrain that threatened to digest her boots.

Tony was sweating when they reached the top. He took a cigarette from his pocket, which he was about to light before the Father stopped him. "They're down there for the rut," he pointed to the valley. "They'll smell that. No shouting and no sudden gestures. Tread carefully and watch out for sticks. A broken twig can scatter them in an instant."

They followed along the flat top of the hill, which curved out to the distance, affording a view of the glen below. There was a plushness to the land on the other side of their climb. Minute variations in microclimate resulted in dramatically different expressions of flora and fauna. Odilio scanned the valley with his binoculars. He could see the group of male and female deers congregating for the rut. Hormone-pumped, half-starved, and teeming with aggression, the stags competed for the affection of the hinds. Now, the excitement was really building in him. For the first time since arriving in Scotland, he was reminded why he loved the place so much.

They walked the plateau of the glenside for a hundred yards until they reached a junction from where they could descend into the valley or climb further up a path leading to a nearby Munro, the peak of which was hidden in a layer of cloud. "We don't want to shoot from any further than a hundred yards, especially with this headwind," said the Father.

"I'd fancy they're a hundred and fifty away," said Phillip, studying the deer through his binoculars.

"One twenty at most," Father Tom replied. "We'll make a descent to station ourselves there on the flat." He pointed to a ridge of grassless earth carved

194

into the side of the hill below them. "Tread very carefully. Those deer will smell everything, and no one wants to break a leg climbing down."

They followed the Father down the hill in a line. Odilio sensed Tabitha's frustration at having to tackle the steep gradient in wellingtons. "Not long, darling," he said. "We just need to find the perfect place, then we can begin." Father Tom reached the ridge first, and without using binoculars, watched the deer closely. The others reached shortly afterwards.

"All good, Father?" asked Phillip.

The Father shook his head and muttered something under his breath.

"What's the problem?" said Tony.

"We can't take any of those," Father Tom said, staring into the valley. "They're all in their prime, I'm afraid."

"Surely we can make an exception?" Tony said, glancing at Phillip, who looked back at the Father.

"Not on this estate," the Father said. "We don't do trophies here, ever." He tapped the floor with his stick as if the matter was settled.

Tony looked to Leroy for a second opinion. "What do you think?" he asked.

Leroy shrugged. "If that's where they put the red tape, what can I say? His deer."

"I wouldn't call it red tape," said Father Tom, rubbing the side of his face in contemplation. "It's how we make the deer last here. It's what makes the

Glendales so great. Head back up. We'll skirt the Munro. There's more deer less than an hour away."

Odilio held Tabitha's hand as they struggled back up the hill. He was anxious her mood would deteriorate any moment, what with the endless walking and waiting around.

"Let's play a game," he suggested. "Do you know 'Catch the Colour'?" One player says a colour and the other has a minute to find as many things as—" A piercing report rang through his body like an electric shock. For a moment he lost his footing and was forced to use his free hand to steady himself against the slope. Tabitha screamed. Father Tom roared:

"What the Jesus was that?" Odilio glanced over his shoulder. Phillip, too, had slipped over, and the tutor was helping him back to his feet. Below, Tony was in hysterics.

"Just checking it worked," he said, pointing the rifle in the air.

"Don't worry, only hit a cloud." The younger gamekeeper laughed; Father Tom did not. He scanned the glen with his binoculars for the resultant movement of the deer.

"They've all bolted," he said. "They'll run into the next valley and unsettle the others there. Chances are, we won't find a thing, now."

"Oh, don't be such a miserable bastard," said Tony, looking to his gamekeeper for approval. "If it's the estate I'm told it is, there'll be deer every fifty yards."

They walked the next half an hour in silence. The prospect of ending the hunt without a kill weighed on Odilio as he carried Tabitha on his shoulders. There was meant to be immense educational value in a stag-less hunt — some maintained you learnt more this way than when you were successful, but it was difficult to believe it when it actually happened. They reached the foot of the Munro and skirted its eastern side, neither gaining nor losing height. The air was still and the sun shone from its highest position. It was still very cold. As they circumvented the small mountain, a deep ravine appeared to their left, from which emanated the sound of running water. "Look!" said Tabitha, from her father's shoulders. "I see deer!"

"Where?" said Odilio. Tabitha pointed to the valley emerging in view. "Oh, she's right. Deer ahead! Deer, look, Tom!"

Father Tom stopped immediately and dropped to the floor. The others crouched in the long grass as he studied the scene through his binoculars. The deer were ahead on the same stretch of land, further down the slope as it descended into marshland. "There's no wind to carry our smell, and the waterfall drowns out our noise," said Phillip, a smile forming on his lips. "Perfect conditions."

"There are good deer, too," said Father Tom. "Some healthy ones we'll want to keep, but a few switches we can take."

Tony required no further instruction. Leroy set up the tripod stand for the rifle as Phillip, too, got to work setting up his position. The tutor stood to one side, watching the men prepare their guns with the enthusiasm of schoolboys playing

197

soldiers. "Look, Tabs," Odilio said, passing her his binoculars. He loaded his rifle and lowered himself to his knees. "What do you see?"

"I can see one... two... three... four... five deers," she paused. "And one... two... three... four... five... six, more. That's..."

"That's eleven deers, Tabitha," said Odilio. "Now, we have to wait for Thomas to tell us which ones are sick — the ones we have to shoot — and which ones are healthy. Thomas can tell the age of a deer just by looking at—" Three shots were fired in quick succession. Odilio covered his ears.

"Got the fucker!" Tony shouted. "Big bastard, too!" He was beaming. "Quick. Take a pop, Phil, before they're all gone."

Phillip took aim with his rifle. It let out one muffled crack. "Missed," he tutted.

"Nevermind," said Tony. "Plenty of meat to go round. How about that, Father, aye?" He looked at Father Tom, who studied the scene through his binoculars with a grim expression.

"You got a perfectly good hind and injured a buck," he said without enthusiasm.

"Thank you," said Tony.

"You weren't meant to shoot the buck. That's exactly what I told you. You've injured him, and he's bolted: now you're going to have to finish him off."

"Right," said Tony, reloading his rifle.

"You won't get him like that," said Father Tom. "He's in the bushes — I think."

Leroy peered through his binoculars. "I see the hind: good shot, just above the foreleg," he said. "I can't see the buck he's talking about. Maybe he's gone into the bushes, or maybe he's bolted for the ditch." The gamekeeper lowered his binoculars. He put a cigarette to his lips and lit it with a match.

"So what do you want me to do?" said Tony.

The gamekeeper looked across the valley, thinking about the deer in the grass. "It's up to the Father, really," he said, blowing a cone of smoke into the air.

Father Tom pulled up his trouser leg and reached for the knife sheathed around his ankle. He handed it to Tony, who took it with a look of bemusement, marvelling privately at its size and weight. "You want me to stab it up?" he laughed at the Father. "I'm a hunter, not some hood rat from Peckham."

"You'll end its life quickly. Slit its throat or pop it through the back of the spine. Did you think you could shoot it at close range? Don't be so silly." The Father looked at Tony contemptuously. Tony looked at Leroy for help, but the gamekeeper said nothing and smoked his cigarette.

"He knows it won't survive and that this is what you have to do. Now, go." Father Tom clapped his hands together.

"Fuck it," said Tony. "You think I've never bled an animal before?" He turned and marched down the hill, clutching the knife in his hand. The others stood where they were.

"It's alright, Tabitha," Odilio said. "Tony's going to put the deer to sleep. It's for the best. We don't want it to suffer anymore."

199

Tony Romano charged down the hill, a confused hatred working through him. The blade seemed to provide his only focus. His mind felt as if it were contained somewhere in his hand or, even, in the membrane of sweat between his palm and the handle. He snarled as he shuffled across the patchy terrain to the body of the hind. Not a bad shot, he thought, nudging the carcass with his foot. Leroy was right: he'd taken it out just above the foreleg. A strange pink fluid bubbled out the entrance wound. He kicked it once more for good luck, then turned back to the valley, to the spectating crowd now a blur on the hill, and grimaced.

It didn't take long to find the blood trail. It made a line through the grass, past the bushes, towards the ditch that led to the stream of running water. Studying the ground ahead, Tony could see no sign of the buck in the neighbouring meadow; it had to be somewhere in the ditch, resting — dying, more likely — between the rocks and clumps of long grass. Tony licked his lips. Striding on his own, unencumbered by the weight of the rifle, he was aware that he was tipsy from all the Scotch he'd put away over the morning. A tipsy that so far had only found its way to his legs. His mind was sharper than it had ever been. He was hungry, too. He thought that he would like to get the business with the deer over, and then head somewhere good for lunch.

Approaching the ditch, he heard the gargled mewls of the downed creature cutting against the peaceful sound of the stream. Tony stared at the landscape surrounding him: there was nothing as far as the eye could see. Whisky commercial footage. A damp desert of grass and razed hillsides. What was the fuss about? Scotland was depressing when you thought about it. Reaching the edge of the stream, Tony found the animal splayed awkwardly on the rocks. The old man was right: his shot had only injured the creature. The bullet seemed to have glanced its belly, shattering its leg on exit. It was as good as dead in a place like this. But now Tony realised what the old man was wrong about. This was no buck, but a fully grown red stag. Two hundred kilos of it, he fancied, and adorned with the largest set of antlers he'd ever seen: symmetrical, thick and perfectly formed, a prize stag of the sort you definitely weren't meant to shoot. What was there left to do? The creature was beyond saving. The old man had given him clear instructions. Tony gripped the knife in his hand and stepped forward. The creature looked up at him. Its glassy eyes stared in resignation: it was giving itself over. He reached forward, pre-empting a final surge of aggression that didn't come. In a second, the deed was done. The blade sliced cleanly through its windpipe. He drew it forward, out its neck, a spurt of blood ejecting to the floor, killing it instantly.

It was Tabitha who first realised what was beside Tony's feet as they made their way to the stream. The fallen hind, which they'd passed on the way, had turned her face pale; the dead stag — its slit throat and surrounding blood pool — set her off in tears. Odilio doubled back as the others drew closer. Phillip and Leroy stood over the stag's body, commenting on its size, while Father Tom scanned the valley and saw something in the emerging clouds that told him the wind had changed. He did not say anything about the stag by the stream until he was asked. "What do we do with it?" said Stuart.

"Not much we can do," said the Father. "Leave it here, I suppose."

"We'll gut it then stick it in the car," said Leroy, overhearing them. "It's a beauty, Tony. One of the finest I've ever seen."

Tony was unable to hide his delight. He took a long drink from his flask. "Shouldn't have taken it, of course," said the Father. "There's no honour in taking something like that."

"I'd say you were a bitter old man," said Tony.

"It's a beauty for sure," Leroy said. "Worth taking as a trophy now it's done. But it shouldn't have been taken like that — the Father's right." Tony glowered at his gamekeeper, then turned to Phillip for his verdict.

"I could call someone to pick it up in the car," said Phillip, removing his deerstalker to scratch his head.

"Can't get a car within three miles of here," said the Father. "Ever tried to shift a five hundred pound carcass across three miles of grassland? Couldn't move it if we wanted to. Couldn't move it if it was worth it."

"We should do something," said Stuart. "Seems a shame to just leave it."

"No other option," said the Father. "If we drag it, we'll mash it up. No trophy in a mashed carcass. Plus, if the boys see it, they'll talk. Beaters claim they're not gossips, but really they are. They'll say we're flexible for the right price. No, this stag stays here."

"Wait one minute, Father," said Leroy. "It's a beauty, whatever you think. Why should we leave it for the crows?"

"It's the rules, Jones."

"Your rules, maybe. At least let us take the head. I agree, the rest isn't worth lifting."

"I guess they could do that," said Phillip.

Tony looked at the gamekeepers, and then glanced over to Odilio. "What do you think?"

Odilio was standing some distance away on the ledge before the stream, an arm around Tabitha, who was shivering from the cold. Any willingness to respond diplomatically had now been exhausted. "I'd listen to Tom if I were you," he said coolly.

Tony snorted. "Well, luckily not many people care what you think anyway. Leroy, give us a hand removing the head will you?"

"You don't listen to anyone," said Odilio. Tony turned, gripping the butt of his rifle. "You never have," Odilio swallowed. "You do whatever you want, and that's why you hurt people. Take the deer, but I don't want to see you ever again, you... *horrible pervert.*"

The others watched in the shock of those who have underestimated the suppressed emotions in an otherwise ordinary display of tension between friends. Tony's pupils turned to pinpricks as he registered Odilio's words. He lunged as soon as that registration was complete, throwing himself forwards, his arms flailing like windmills, while the others fought to hold him back.

Odilio led Tabitha back the way they had come as the curses fired from the scramble behind. Something in him had, at once, been put right. He drew his first deep breath in weeks. The sort of breath the Yogis talk about, which grounds you in the present and dissolves life's worries away. "Let's go," he said, squeezing

Tabitha's hand. "We've seen quite enough here."

Had they turned around at that moment, they would have witnessed Tony

disentangle himself from the barrier of men and retreat to the slain deer. They

would have watched him reach for the bloodied knife on the ground next to its slit

throat, watched as he stood over the limp carcass, adjusting the position of its head,

using its antler to tilt it forward, before feeling around for its vertebral columns,

lining the blade up with the gap between its bones. Next, they would have seen him

raise the knife in anger, above the intended entrance point, clasping the handle,

cursing the dead creature, cursing others, too, perhaps the very heavens, before

bringing it down into the animal with his full chaotic force.

Then, they would witness other things. Things that would happen quickly.

Things they would come to understand in different ways. Those things might be

explained to them later as such: that ion gradients can reside in oxygen-starved

nerve cells. A last gasp of consciousness supervening on a sparkle of impulses. It

was the guttural sound of the deer that made Odilio and Tabitha turn around,

overriding their best intentions to look away. Life surrendering itself to the levelling

of free energy: the discharge of static would manifest as one final and violent

action. Bucking its head back was a retort to the blade's insertion. Where Tony's

crotch was there was now the stag. It happened quickly. Odilio fumbled to cup his

daughter's ears as they looked to this new wound, the frothing red proliferating

through the white wool jumper. What a strange conjunction, they thought, as his knees buckled and his eyes rolled back into his head. There was a short silence.

Before long, new sounds emitted in a chorus, filling the glen with ghosts.

29

The Airbus A320 took off from Nice exactly on time. The plane ascended quickly but comfortably to cruising altitude within ten minutes. It was a cloudless day; the aircraft afforded magnificent views of the peaks of the Rhone-Alpes below. Helena paid no attention to the views, nor to the paperback she'd picked up at the airport bookshop. One thing was on her mind, and it was Elias. Elias was in trouble; Elias was trouble. Elias was lost, and they should search for him; Elias was a lost cause and needed to do some serious soul-searching. Back and forth, her anxieties flipped. Seven miles up in the sky, there was no chance of getting through to him. Perhaps this sort of binge was typical. Was she just elongating her humiliation by working herself into a panic? He'd be back tomorrow, dishevelled and high, like he'd been on the way there. He'd collect his passport from the guest house and get a driver to take him to the airport, where he could sort his own way back. It was time to give up worrying.

But fifty unanswered calls and texts said otherwise. Helena was starting to regret some of those earlier ones, much spikier in tone — quite mean when you reread them. Nonetheless, once they made contact, it would be on those she'd rely upon to convince him she was in on his little stunt. Ruin everything, disappear, get fucked, and then come crawling back expecting a kiss on the forehead. *Hey, please call. I'm getting worried Xx.* Those were embarrassing, but they covered other bases, too, not that she wanted to think about them yet.

The idea of Ingrid calling had crossed her mind more than once. What would Helena say? If she was going to be honest about leaving France minus Elias, she'd need to be honest about her reasons why. But that would require relaying all the gory details of the weekend: details she could hardly expect the old Swede to handle well. For Ingrid, responsibility lay with everyone but her son. For now, it was best to avoid contaminating their face-off with outsiders. He might get back to her tonight — that wasn't so unlikely. Then Helena could get back to it. The drafted message for the Karlsson family lawyer that specified the precise legal clauses under which she was terminating their contract was sitting unsent in her inbox. She just wanted to know he was OK. Then they could brush this sorry episode under the rug and move on with their lives. Helena put on her eye mask and tried her best to fall asleep for the three-hour flight to Scotland.

30

"Phone a fucking ambulance," Tony gnashed, a thick spittle forming around the cracks of his mouth, as he pulled up clumps of grass around him and tossed them desperately in the air.

"I'm trying, I'm trying," Phillip gulped.

"Me too," said the tutor. "There's no signal at all."

"Well… find some fucking signal." Tony's eyeballs followed them one by one, casting intense, accusing, hate-filled looks. Then he passed out for a fourth time, providing some temporary respite to the situation.

"It's hopeless," said the tutor.

"We're going to need to go back."

"And call an ambulance there?"

"Can't get a car three miles near," murmured the Father, who was clearing his throat of residual sick.

"I'll call an air ambulance at the house," said Stuart. "I can run."

"Go, then," said Phillip. "Get one of my men to talk to them: they can provide our exact location."

"Fuck," Tony screamed, coming to once more.

"We're getting help as soon as we can," Phillip said with a quivering voice as the tutor made for the hill they'd come from, with a quick and convincing jog.

After the stag's antlers had found themselves embedded in Tony, no one had moved. Then, one by one, each reacted in their unique, varyingly-useful way. The Father's reaction had been perhaps the most surprising. For a man who had spent his life in the business of killing, it was revealing to witness his squeamishness at the ravaging of human flesh. He had thrown up several times before they'd even attempted to take Tony's trousers off; the sight of his partially disgorged genitalia when they did had made him faint. He had crawled off to a mound some distance from the group, where he'd stayed since, occasionally inputting to the matter in a feeble, pitiful voice that seemed desperate to be anywhere but here.

Phillip had kept it together. His concerns pertained to the bureaucratic and the incriminating. It was not a good look having someone with such an injury on your land: much worse if they bled to death following the failure of four adults to secure an ambulance in time. In the meantime, he was doing his best to console the patient. Whenever Tony came to, it was Phillip who tried to talk him into calm — a task the others had quietly given up on. Stuart's interests were in securing the ambulance and he'd already proved himself to this end by running the distance back to the house. Odilio's concerns had narrowed to Tabitha. He had taken her away from the scene, to the nearby brook, where he reassured her that the situation was in control. He worried about the impact of witnessing such violence on her young mind, yet she seemed to be doing okay given the circumstances. The sight of the slaughtered deer, Odilio noticed, had appeared to set her off worse than the castration of Tony.

It was an hour until they heard anything. Then, they heard it in the distance: the rumblings of an engine, rising in pitch then falling, grumbling and groaning over the bumpy land, until it appeared in sight. "Stuart!" Phillip ejected, rising from his hands and knees as the motorbike approached them. By now, the situation had entered a new phase. They had done their best to keep pressure on the wound, but Tony had lost lots of blood. He was becoming groggy and incoherent in the increasingly rarer moments he was awake. Lapses in consciousness now worried the remaining party, to which Odilio had rejoined safe in the knowledge his old friend was incapable of retaliation, but also, out of an emerging fear Tony would die on them. The motorbike sped across the last stretch of the field and it was only then that they could make out its second passenger. Stuart parked and jumped off; Rachel chased after him. "The helicopter's on its way," he shouted.

"I've got first responder training," added Rachel, who was carrying a first aid kit with her. "I'm going to try and stabilise him."

Rachel's professionalism was on display from that moment. Despite having walked into what looked like the aftermath of a battle — the rifles scattered across the floor; the slaughtered animals, and semi-conscious patient, bleeding into the grass — she remained calm and level-headed. Her competence was contagious, as she instructed Stuart to lift Tony's legs, cleaning and applying pressure to the wound with a medical-grade towel. The Father, Odilio, and Phillip, who knew only the sport of violence, watched as she performed this miracle of healing. She pressed on the wound with a force the others had been incapable of maintaining, appreciating the necessary pressure for the injury. Tony was reawakened by this interruption. He shouted in confusion at the appearance of the unfamiliar face. It was only some minutes later that he evidenced any sign of revival. "While you're down there," he murmured, lifting his head to watch the procedure.

"Shhh," said Rachel as she pushed it back down. "Say nothing. Keep still. Try to relax."

The Father commandeered the air ambulance to the meadow. A team of paramedics took over where Rachel left off. "You did great," said Stuart, wrapping his arm around her, as she rejoined the party, spectating from some distance away. For fifteen minutes, Tony was occluded by medical personnel as various pipes and apparatus were stuffed in and around him. Then, he was stretchered to the helicopter, before one of the paramedics came over to tell the onlookers someone would have to accompany him to the hospital. Odilio looked around. Despite his misgivings, it would be unfair to proffer anyone else for the task but himself. He kissed Tabitha on the cheek and told the others he would rejoin them later. "You were fantastic, Rachel," Odilio shouted.

"Thank you," Rachel waved back at him. "Good luck!"

Two minutes later, he was in the sky, looking down at the muddy desert of deer-razed grass. The estate mansion stood proudly as the only building for miles. It looked like a playhouse from such a height: there was something childish in the design. It was how a child might imagine a house, with its cube shape and square windows, and everything in neat, straight lines. There was more land around than anyone could use in a lifetime. It was an immature conception of space, rendering the landscape into a sterilised facsimile of nature. Odilio glanced at Tony, who was now safely unconscious. He felt nothing looking at his old friend rigged up with oxygen. He sensed he'd moved on. Now, it was time to tell the world the good news.

He wrote it during the ride to the hospital. He read through it once to correct the misspellings, but there was little in its tone or message he felt necessary to edit. The words had existed in him long before that moment. He screenshotted the message from the notes app of his phone and shared the image on Twitter. It read:

For too long, I looked up to Tony, ignoring the deplorable behaviour I witnessed to the benefit of my career. Like many men in this industry, I propagated an atmosphere of indifference to sexual abuse and harassment, which allowed a sexual predator to thrive without repercussions. I am disgusted with myself for my years of silence. I am disgusted with Tony. Any respect I ever had for him is null and voided in light of recent circumstances. From the bottom of my heart, I am sorry to everyone I let down.

Odilio hit send just as the helicopter began to descend onto the hospital. Tony was rushed to an emergency ward. "He's lost a lot of blood," one of the paramedics told Odilio, who was racing in tow.

"I'm not surprised," said Odilio, panting behind. "He was bleeding out for over an hour. None of us knew what to do."

"How did it happen?"

"He was headbutted by a stag," said Odilio. "Antler straight to the crotch. We thought the animal was dead, but apparently not."

"Happens all the time," said the paramedic. "They're rarely as dead as you think. One last surge as you go to cut them up. You'd be surprised how many eyeballs go missing around here. Don't worry, though, he's going to be fine."

Tony was taken into surgery. The doctors explained that the procedure would likely take several hours. Odilio signed a form that detailed his contact information in case anything went wrong. He drank a cup of tea from the hospital cafe, and then he was allowed to go. He ordered a taxi. It was drizzling when he left. Odilio looked out the window for the drive home. A weight had been lifted, and he was enjoying the feeling of its release. He watched the countryside with a sense of peace. It was time to call Helena and confess everything.

31

"We're as good as done," said Father Tom, holding his head in his hands. They were sitting around the fireplace in one of the many rooms of the Glendales, watching as the flames flickered against the ancient hearth. "Shouldn't have taken that animal," he repeated, groaning as he stretched his legs. Phillip poured the Father some whisky. The Father stared at his feet. He'd been a babbling wreck all afternoon, repeating himself as he put away drink after drink. Phillip was taken aback (and privately amused) by this rare lapse of his gamekeeper's stoicism. For Phillip, there remained only rationality in response to such a situation. It was no use getting flustered. He would ready his team of lawyers if and when charges were pressed (he was confident the grounds to sue would be invalidated by the prosecution having breached certain rules of the estate; drinking alcohol on a hunt, for instance, was expressly prohibited). Even still, there was nothing to gain in worrying now. It was a quality he'd picked up from his father: fortitude as a response to adversity. An unflinching resolve in the face of the gruesome. Sure, he'd struggled out in the field, when the adrenaline was flowing and the situation demanded a degree of critical thinking. But now, feet up by the fireplace, a beef joint roasting away in the kitchen, he was feeling fine again.

"The boy did good today," said Phillip, cutting through the festering silence.

"The teacher lad?" the Father said, looking at him with bright eyes. "Aye, he did a good job." The two men nodded in agreement.

"For a man who doesn't shoot, he wasn't afraid to get his hands dirty," said Phillip.

"He did well." The Father paused and thought for a while. "And that lass," he added. "She done well, too."

"I think she saved his life."

"Aye." The Father looked into the fireplace. "Should never have taken that animal," he said, finishing the contents of his glass, then lurching forward for his scarf. "One of the boys will see it unless I can get there and bury it first." He took his coat from the hanger. "I'll head out at first light, not that it matters, though. There's going to be a scandal surrounding that moron. Not a good look for us, an injury like that. Not good for business."

"There's nothing to fear, now," said Phillip. "What's done is done. We'll weather the storm we have coming. The Glendales have fared worse."

"I hope you're right," said the old hunter. "Still, it's bad luck for us. You know it's a curse to witness a man's castration? I'll burn some sage in the fireplace tomorrow morning. Are you going to be alright on your own?"

"I'll be fine," smiled Phillip. His phone beeped and he checked the message. "My sister arrives in fifteen minutes."

"Well, goodnight," the Father waved as he left the room. "I'm going to try to sleep it off."

"Good night," said Phillip. He let out a long exhalation once his gamekeeper had gone. "What a fucking day."

*

The gravel crackled as the car pulled into the drive. The throb of the engine, which could be heard throughout the house, cut dead and a pair of doors opened and closed in succession. The car boot was lifted, luggage was piled on the noisy shingle, then the boot was shut with a bang. "Mummy!" Tabitha was the first to greet her as she stepped through the door. Helena hugged her as Phillip's staff flocked to collect her luggage.

"My baby," Helena cooed. "What a brave girl you are." She kissed Tabitha on the ear and squeezed her tightly. "What a rotten day it's been darling, you must be exhausted."

Tabitha shook her head. "I'm not tired, actually," she said.

"You're a hero, then," said Helena.

"Rachel was the real hero," Tabitha turned to the staircase, where Stuart and Rachel had gathered at the top. "She saved him."

"I know, I heard everything, darling," Helena said, blowing a kiss to the pair. "You've all been heroes while I was away. You've all done fantastically."

Phillip bound into the hallway. As soon as he saw his sister, his face changed. "So good to see you, Boo," he gasped as they embraced each other. "Welcome to the Glendales. It's been a long time."

"It was February last year, I believe."

"A long time." Phillip grinned, flashing his crooked teeth.

216

"Some of us work, you know?" Helena smiled.

"You've worked quite enough, Boo. Things fell to pieces while you were gone. I guess it really is the start of the holidays now."

"Rotten business with the stag," Helena said sympathetically.

"So you've heard?"

"Odilio called me on the way. What an idiot my husband is for taking that man with you."

"Rotten day," Phillip smiled. "Your husband will be back soon. I'm quite shattered. Let's have an early dinner."

Odilio arrived fifteen minutes later. He entered the front door, kissed Helena on both cheeks, and shared a knowing look with Phillip, who went to check the progress of the beef joint. "Hello," said Helena, her tone morphing into something more serious as they found themselves alone.

"How are you?" Odilio asked. He was thinking about how beautiful Helena looked and how much he'd missed her. It was rare they spent more than a night apart, and on the occasions they did, it provided an opportunity to reset his appreciation for the little things he took for granted.

"We need to talk," said Helena.

"Sure," said Odilio.

"Shall we go upstairs?"

"Of course," he nodded. After filling Helena in on the events of the weekend, she'd reacted by hanging up the phone, explaining, before she did, that she was confused why he'd felt the need to lie to her. Why pretend he'd told Tony he was moving on? He'd spent the remainder of the taxi journey thinking about how to defend himself on this point. But stepping out of the taxi, walking up the gravel drive to the house, Odilio was reminded that the days of defending his behaviour were over. He did not want to play the role of his own advocate any longer. He would say sorry and tell her, right now, things were going to be different.

"Elias is missing," she said, as she closed the bedroom door. She sat down on the armchair next to the bed. Odilio perched on the end of the duvet.

"Missing?" he said. Relief the conversation didn't involve him was quickly replaced by new concerns. "So he didn't fly back with you?"

"He was meant to. I've been trying to reach him. He went out — Lord knows where — no one's seen him since. I've tried calling. None of the Walkers' staff have seen him. His passport is still in his room."

"Where could he have gone?"

"No idea," said Helena. "He doesn't have any friends there, as far as I know, but he has more money than he knows what to do with — look…" Her voice trailed off as she reached into her bag. She took out her phone and showed Odilio the headline of a Swedish tabloid a friend had sent her. She clicked 'translate'. It read: ELIAS, SON OF INGRID, IN COCAINE BINGE AT FRENCH STRIPCLUB. It was accompanied with several photographs of the young artist, snorting lines off a table, surrounded by a googly-eyed group of teenagers, as a woman in her underwear caressed his thigh. "Ingrid is going to go mental when she sees this," said Helena. "They're such a secretive family; this isn't good for them."

Odilio took the phone and scrolled through. "Jesus," he said. "Cocaine and strippers. I bet Sylvie Dupont is delighted that's how he's spending her money."

"He didn't get any of her money," said Helena. "He didn't exactly work his charms. She thought he was weird."

"So you came back on your own?"

Helena nodded. "What else could I do?"

"Did you call the police?"

"I checked. The person has to be missing for seventy-two hours, or there has to be a good reason to think something's wrong."

"I'm sure he's fine, of course," said Odilio. "But it's good to cover every base."

"I'm terrified his mother will get in contact."

"You're not his babysitter."

"To Ingrid, I am. I should never have come back. I thought if I went to the airport it would somehow call his bluff. What the hell could he be doing?"

Odilio ran a hand through his hair and thought. "Contact the consulate. Take it as seriously as you can, as early as possible. Once it's been seventy-two hours, file a missing person report. I'm sure he's just out having a good time."

"He really was a liability," Helena said. "I looked like an idiot. Luckily, Elizabeth is an old friend, but otherwise, I can't afford to compromise my reputation like that again. When the exhibition is over, I'll drop him. I want to work with a woman next — I'm sick of spoiled men."

"Speaking of," said Odilio, with a naughty grin. It was a look Helena was familiar with.

"What a day," she said, shaking her head. "You know, I don't give a shit about Tony."

"I'm just sorry I lied to you."

"Mhmm."

"I didn't know how to get rid of him. I fluffed it. I guess I needed more time." Odilio dropped to his knees. He crawled forward and kissed her hands. "You're a wonderful person," he said. "The sweetest, the most charming, the best."

"Am I really?" her tone invited him to continue.

"*Really*," he said. "Tony is a cretin. You were right about that."

"I know," said Helena. "Such a shame Tabitha had to see all that, though."

"It'll build resilience, I guess. She handled it well."

"What will the children at school think? They'll say she really does grow up in a house of dinosaurs — shooting holidays, guns, and gorings."

"Let them say what they like." He kissed her hands again.

32

The following morning, Helena drove Tabitha to Inverness for a day of shopping
and a trip to the castle. Phillip was away on the sort of vague business that occupied
rural aristocrats. Stuart and Rachel were off hiking the surrounding countryside.
Odilio was home alone. He'd use the opportunity to finish his Blue Langoustine
piece. Sitting at the desk in the study, reading through the notes he'd taken of the
lunch, he was aware he had nothing worthwhile to say about the experience. As a
piece of journalism, he could muster no more than a shoddy regurgitation — a
Franken monster of cliche, for want of an interesting take of his own. And yet, there
was another angle he was considering: something he wanted to get off his chest,
which the piece could provide an opportunity to vent. He'd use his atypical
experience to subvert the usual formula of his column. Sitting at the large desk, with
its view of the valley, he wrote without pause, his energy springing from a new
well. He drafted 1300 words, made a pot of tea, and then revised them, repeating the
process until he was happy. It was dark when he finished. Resisting the temptation
to overthink, he emailed the piece to his editor, then dragged himself to the living
room, rooting himself by the fire, quietly contented as he closed his eyes.

It was an ode to good company:

*It doesn't matter how fine an establishment is if we're not sharing the table
with the right company. No configuration of napkins, cutlery, or table cloths can
make up for a lousy conversation; no special cooking method or expensive*

ingredient can, alone, create the escapist fantasy that a restaurant — for the one or two hours we're sat within its walls — provides us with. Dinner with the wrong person brings the entire experience down with it. Dinner with the right person can elevate the most mediocre canteen to an unforgettable dining sensation. Food is smoke and mirrors: we project our feelings of comfort, security, love, and compassion onto it, which, in turn, creates the flavour. No one who has just received bad news will enjoy a mouthful of fine food. Likewise, a simple boiled potato tastes like heaven in the hungry, happy mouth. I learnt this at the Blue Langoustine in Aviemore, where I was subjected to the worst lunch in my career as a food journalist, which, fortunately for this well-respected establishment, had absolutely nothing to do with them.

Cooper called an hour later. The call roused Odilio from a nap. "Odilio," his editor shouted down the phone with trademark enthusiasm. "What's the weather like in Scotland?" Small talk ensued about the rain; an anecdote about setting crayfish traps in Wales during a hail storm was recounted by his editor, who told the story clumsily, skipping key details that ruined the punchline "Anyway," said Cooper. "Just received your copy… What's it all about?"

Odilio cleared his throat. "What's what all about?"

"Bit of an odd one, don't you think?"

Odilio chewed the end of his thumb. "Sorry, Cooper, but take it or leave it. There was really nothing else I could say."

"I told you to pull something special out the bag. Remember our chat last month? You wanted to bring the old Odilio back."

222

"I know," Odilio grumbled. "Although, I didn't exactly hold back. It was a dreadful lunch."

"It's too airy-fairy. Readers don't want philosophising in a restaurant column. I know you're on holiday, so I'll have to let it go, but we want some solids next week."

"You'll get your solids," Odilio muttered.

"One more thing: what do you want to do about this ten bird roast thing? The agent's hassling Amy and you're not telling her anything. She hasn't heard a word from you all week. If you don't want it, hand it to someone else. You don't seem very excited, and I don't want to waste anyone's time."

"Please, pass it on."

"I hope you don't mind."

"Not at all," said Odilio, hanging up the phone.

The past had no real existence, Odilio thought, nesting in the armchair. There was only a malleable, plural, and diverging impression of what had been. It was an illusion. The answers didn't lie in the glow of nostalgia. When he was a young man there hadn't been any golden years to hark back to. That's when he'd put his best foot forward, unencumbered by a vision of what should be. And the past: how good had it really been? Wasn't it clear, now, how much editing went on in the creation of memory? Each told their story casting himself in the best light. But dredging up just a piece of the past had taught Odilio it was senseless to wed yourself to an idealised version of events. Nostalgia was a trick. He would focus on

223

the present, retaining an unspecified optimism about the future: that's how he would foster the new experiences he craved now.

Odilio fell asleep again. One of the kitchen staff woke him to ask if he wanted some soup. He replied with ambiguous grogginess. Ten minutes later, she placed a bowl of minestrone next to him. He woke again and tucked into it hungrily. It was delicious. He checked his phone just before six o'clock, just as his family was pulling into the drive. He had a new message from Tony. He paused, wondering if he should read it, before deciding to block the number right away.

33

The call came through in the middle of the night and woke them. Normally, Helena's phone was set to silent. There was something alien about the unfamiliar, crescendoing ringtone that worked its way, first, into their dreams and, then, into reality as the gravity of its meaning awoke them in a confused panic. Helena scrambled for the bedside. "Hello?" — her voice husky and filled with sleep. A voice on the other end of the line. "Ca va?" A tremble. Odilio sat up in bed. He did not have to understand French to know the severity of what had happened. Helena spoke in short sentences, increasingly starved for breath. "Oh, mon dieu... No... Mon dieu...". As soon as she hung up, she burst into tears as Odilio comforted her in his arms. It was some time before he asked her exactly what had happened, although part of him already knew.

They found Elias in the marina. Witness reports corroborated themselves, and a picture had quickly come to light. Elias had met a group of social media influencers at a strip club in Nice. He'd bought a stash of drugs to share with them: a toxicology examination would later confirm high quantities of cocaine and MDMA in his system. Later that night, he joined them on a private yacht for a party. Around four in the morning, he'd taken up a dare to swim back to the mainland, but in the end, no one had checked in on the progress of the wager. The whole thing had been forgotten by the remaining party, which was not, after all, a teetotal affair. Elias never made it to the mainland. He was thirty-two years old.

Odilio held Helena through the night: unable to fall back asleep, his mind raced with thoughts. His brain worked like a hammer, pummeling the recent events against the anvil of the news, that showed up his own woes as a kind of self-obsessive privilege. As dawn broke, a series of truths precipitated in his mind he'd perhaps always understood but which were now clearer in their distillation. Life was precious. There was a limit to pleasure. Beyond that limit, its pursuit caused disproportional and unnecessary pain. Shooting a deer, for instance: was it ever worth it? How could the high of making the shot justify the snuffing out of a life? But humans are hoarders, Odilio thought. Greedy, pathological: they struggle to step aside in their accumulation of more to let others pass unmolested. Redemption lies in taking just enough and letting the rest go. Make giving a habit. Sate the same nature with the liberation of refusing to chase the illusory highs of more.

In the morning, Rachel and Stuart were driven to the station without explanation, other than that the family had received tragic news and needed time alone. Phillip gave his staff the day off so that they could have some privacy in the house. They agreed not to tell Tabitha the news for fear of overwhelming her. They were lucky that Tabitha was still at an age where the moods of her parents weren't so obvious. She still retained the childish notion that one's parents were invincible, that they were unencumbered by the erratic rhythms of feeling children are subjected to daily. And so Odilio and Helena were able to hide their diminished energy and sapped confidence — the general spirit of melancholy that hung over their early dinner, where Tabitha announced with excitement that, from now on, she would never eat the flesh of an animal, nor use products that caused harm to one.

226

"I'm a vegan," she said as if about to burst with pride. They received the news with ostensible enthusiasm and agreed they would encourage her decision to the best of their ability.

34

"Another coke?" Odilio asked, finishing his beer and looking across the table at Tabitha.

"Please," she said. She was sucking the ice cubes of her last one and spitting them back into the glass like bullets. Odilio ordered a round of drinks then returned his attention to his notebook. Tabitha watched curiously as he jotted things down. "What are you writing, dad?" she asked.

"I'm making an account of our lunch. I don't want to forget anything when we leave. But I have to be discreet; they'll be too nice to us if they know who I am."

Tabitha thought for a second. "But that's a good thing?"

Odilio smiled. "It was good enough, though, wasn't it? They don't need to do anything more."

"It was yummy," said Tabitha, kicking her legs in excitement as a coca-cola was placed on the table in front of her.

"Cheers," said Odilio, taking his beer.

The Pickled Aubergine — the talk of the town. The flagship restaurant of two Palestinian brothers, right in the heart of London. Fresh, seasonal vegan food served with minimal fuss. A concept oft championed but rarely delivered. The food had been exceptionally good. For the starter, they'd had a plate of poached peppers seasoned with garlic and herbs. Next, a delightfully rich soup of onions — a dish that revealed a quality to the ingredient Odilio had spent a lifetime missing. For the main course, miso-glazed aubergines were served with black rice and a fermented cucumber salad. He'd been astounded by the meaty texture and complex flavours of the aubergines, scarcely believing a vegetable could taste so good. They'd finished lunch with a peach crumble. Now, Odilio was making some last-minute notes on the restaurant's ambience and decor. Outside, it was a clear day in November. The trees were filled with copper leaves that cut zig-zagging lines across the clear sky. Odilio finished his notes and nursed his beer in the peace of the afternoon downtime. They walked back to the house via the park, stopping on the way to watch a troop of rollerbladers perform a choreographed dance to a boombox blaring disco funk.

Rachel was in the kitchen when they returned to the house. "I'm so sorry," said Odilio. "I completely forgot you were coming this afternoon." The au pair was on her phone at the kitchen island, drinking a cup of tea. "How long have you been waiting?"

"Not long at all," she smiled. "I've been quite happy here, actually. How are you Tabs? Did you have a nice lunch with your dad?"

"I did," said Tabitha. "It was delicious."

"What are you two going to do, then?" said Odilio.

"I want to colour in," said Tabitha.

"We can do that."

"Let me get my pens!" she called as she raced upstairs.

Odilio and Rachel stood opposite each other in the kitchen. The silence was interrupted by Odilio. "Any news on Stuart?" he asked. Shortly after Scotland, the tutor had been offered a full-time role with a wealthy Parisian family. The salary was un-turndownable and with a great deal of apologising, he'd gone the same week. There'd been no contract in place to stop him. After the incident in Scotland, there was little they felt they could do to bargain him to stay. His departure had been amicable.

"He's actually back this weekend," said Rachel. "He's doing French classes at the Sorbonne. I think he's getting on well." She paused, and asked: "How's Tony?"

"Okay, I think," Odilio said, staring at the oranges in the fruit bowl. "I haven't spoken to him actually. A nurse called recently to tell me they saved one of his testicles, which is good."

"That is good," Rachel smiled.

"He might have to wear special pants or something."

Rachel swallowed. "I only recently found out who he is, by the way."

"That we were on telly together?"

"Yeah," Rachel winced. "And all the other stuff, too."

"You didn't recognise him in Scotland?"

"No," said Rachel. "I didn't follow the news. Stuart told me everything when we got back. I regretted feeling as sorry for him as I did."

Odilio looked at her. "I should have said something."

"Well, it wouldn't have changed anything."

"I shouldn't have let him in the house. I don't know what I was thinking, taking him with us. He sort of sprung out of nowhere."

"He's an old friend, no?"

"We go back years," Odilio nodded.

"So not exactly from nowhere."

"Of course," said Odilio. "It's just I didn't know he'd be *there* exactly. I couldn't get rid of him, to be honest."

"No one ever holds themselves accountable with these things," Rachel said, looking Odilio in the eye. "Everyone wants to wash their hands of him now, but they didn't say anything for years."

"I completely agree," said Odilio. "We entertained him."

"What I don't understand is why the loyalty? Was it so hard to say something earlier?"

Odilio scratched his chin. "He made a lot of people rich…" His voice trailed off. "I didn't know what to do."

"I guess we all miss chances," Rachel said, the usual, amiable expression returning to her face.

"But I want to make it right," said Odilio.

"That's good," said Rachel. "But the chance is gone."

Tabitha walked in, clutching her pencil case and colouring book. "Great work, Tabs," said Rachel. "Where should we draw?"

"Can we put a movie on and sit in the TV room?" she asked. Rachel looked at Odilio for his approval.

"Go ahead," he said. "I'll be in my study."

*

On the other side of the city, Helena Courtenay was stepping into a taxi, making a mental check that she'd said all the important goodbyes before giving the driver her address. As the car made its way through the east London traffic, the tension in her body began to disappear. She undid the buttons of her black Stella McCartney blazer, loosened her belt, and relaxed into the car seat. The adrenaline of the occasion was wearing off and a new exhaustion was taking over. Her mouth was dry as leather: she hadn't drunk water in hours, and her eyes felt tired and strained. She shut them. The balls of her feet ached, as did her jaw from all the talking — incessant talking to fill silences. Silences that feel criminal on such occasions.

The funeral had taken place in Sweden the week before. A close-knit, family affair — the recent outpouring of media attention towards the Karlssons' had pushed this already secretive family practically into hermitage. But the bulk of Elias' social circle existed here in London. Today was the memorial service for those who weren't invited or couldn't make the ceremony in Malmö. In a quiet corner of Tower Hamlets, a ragtag group of mourners had come together to pay their respects. Artists, writers, junkies, and poets. Old flames and new. Unburdened by the company of the deceased's family — free to grieve as they pleased.

Now, everyone was on the same page with the life of Elias Karlsson. The world had come to understand the young artist differently — Helena included. Context always did provide a quick route to forgiveness. The drinking and the drugs; the perpetual disappointment. It all made sense, now. Who wouldn't turn to such methods of escape having endured a childhood like that? Lonely boarding houses; an abusive father and emotionally unavailable mother. It had surprised

232

Helena to read of Ingrid's ongoing oxymorphone abuse. The portrait of the family that came to light was one of negligence, cruelty, and a profound lack of love. The misfits here made a substitute clan. They gathered together to grieve like a real family. Helena held the late Elias in new regard.

And so did the world. One Swedish newspaper had acquired his diaries, as well as a collection of letters to his friends. They were published without the permission of the family, causing a legal storm in his home country. The documents revealed a mind tortured by insecurity. A person who never felt they'd done enough. His own worst critic. On several occasions, he decried the money that he felt poisoned the industry, suggesting to a friend that blowing it all on drugs was the best thing he could do with an undeserved fortune. The attitude that came through in the diary was of someone striving for better — someone constantly on the lookout to exceed their own expectations. Never looking back, never content to stupify in self-contentment. Helena had read everything that came out, appreciating that many of his ideas, it turned out, had far deeper foundations than she'd taken them for. She learnt, too, there was depth to his proposition to her. Her name wasn't mentioned often, but one line caught the attention of the press. 'My Special H: mentor, friend, muse. I love her.' It prompted a tangential discourse over the state of his love life, and the open question: who was Special H? Helena didn't feel a need to input on the matter. She would keep the episode in Elizabeth's garden to herself.

Indeed, the publication of Elias Karlsson's papers put to bed an alternative press reading of his life — one that would have dragged him through the mud for his vices, making public the gory details of his binges with the relish of a voyeur.

233

Instead, Elias would be remembered in the spirit of the great artists before him. A victim of his genius; a body unable to keep up with its mind. A flame that burnt too fiercely and went out too soon.

It did a world of good for his value. It always does. When an artist passes, the quantity of their work is capped, and so its value can no longer be diluted. There's an emotional factor to the process, too. Death allows the artist to transmute into something bigger than the corporeal entity. People can devote themselves to the dead. Dying is the price you pay for a higher kind of love: a forgiving love, almost impossible to forge with the living.

Surrounded by the various players of Elias' short life, Helena had taken to the pulpit of this otherwise secular service in a Stepney church, speaking lovingly of the man she regretfully hadn't known long enough. At the end of the speech, she announced she was setting up a foundation in his honour. The Elias Trust would support members of the artistic community struggling with mental health and drug issues. Seed money for the trust would come through the auctioning of several of Elias' unreleased pieces. Helena had committed to paying five per cent of her profits to the trust on any of his work sold in the forthcoming years.

A number of people came forward to thank her at the drinks event afterwards. There were several offers to contribute to her charitable venture. No one, it seemed, took issue with her over the events leading to Elias' death. She doubted they were even aware she was the last person at the service to have seen the artist alive. Ingrid could take her unfounded blame with her to the grave: Helena wouldn't lose any sleep. It was inevitable, as details of Elias' dysfunctional life came to light, the family would retaliate by pointing the finger more emphatically at those around them. Death was a funny old affair, Helena thought. Everything is thrown in the air when someone dies; it lands in a different place afterwards. It could take years to work out exactly how things would change. After doing the rounds of his friends and more distant relations, she had hung around for half an hour, chatting to a Polish drag queen who'd known Elias in Krakow, before calling the taxi that was now taking her back to her house.

Helena was still holding the sheet of paper on which her eulogy was written. She unfolded it, and reread a section at random:

"Let's go to France!": Elias' words that, for me, summarise the man best. We'd missed our flight to Nice, and he was furious. He wanted to be in France: he wanted to get on with the job and make the best of the situation. That was Elias. He threw himself into everything with the same tenacity; you only have to look at his work. "Let's go to France!". How Churchillian in its sentiment. Although I was his 'patron', Elias was very much a leader. A casualty in battle, where victory is claimed in the legacy he leaves in this room…

Helena folded the piece of paper up and slipped it into her clutch bag. They were driving along the embankment. A light rain had started to fall over the city.

*

Rachel shut the front door and skipped down the wet stone steps to the street. At the end of the road, she took a left down a cobbled mews, where Stuart was waiting for her under an umbrella, his familiar silhouette cutting a solid presence against the

London brume. "Bonne soiree, mon cher," he said, kissing her on each cheek. She stood looking at him, her expression one of admiration until she started laughing.

"You've shaved your beard so short," she stroked his chin. With his free hand, he touched her shoulder then, gently, the side of her face, which he held for the minute or so duration of their kiss. They were horny as they walked down the mews together, hand in hand, reverting to small talk about his journey as they strode with renewed energy that testified to their excitement about the weekend ahead.

"How's our favourite family?" Stuart asked, after delivering a lengthy exposition of the various characters within his Eurostar carriage.

"Same old," said Rachel. "Odilio has cheered up a bit since Scotland, weirdly."

"He's happy to see the back of me?"

"You're not that important," she laughed. "Although he did ask about you earlier."

"Oh yeah? He knows we're together?"

"No. I haven't told them anything, yet. They think we're just good friends."

Stuart squeezed her hand. "Well, we are, aren't we?"

Rachel looked up to the drizzling sky. "I told him you were going to French classes — that was about it. I don't know what you're up to half the time."

"There's not much to say," he nodded. "I'm busy. It's intense. I guess you have to think about the money and see it as a means to an end."

"I want to know more about this family: Les Allards."

236

"What do you want to know," said Stuart, placing his arm around her shoulder.

"Well, what's their story? What are they like?"

"It's always the same story," he said, as they stopped at the pedestrian crossing. "All these families are the same. I mean, you get better and worse ones, but the essentials are there."

"Which are?" said Rachel, teasingly. "Don't forget I basically do the same job as you — they just pay you more and call you a tutor. We're babysitters, really."

Stuart chuckled. "Well, then, you'll know what I'm going to say. These families are haunted by the realisation that their money can only give them so much. I'm not stupid, I know money provides a significantly better quality of life than having none. But there's always a limit, right? In the end, you need a greater sense of purpose than just having stuff. Community, creativity, a sense of humour — these things are missing with the Allards. They know they lack something, but they don't know what it is, or they refuse to accept it's something they can't buy."

"Would you say the same about the Courtenays?"

"Yeah," said Stuart. "Odilio, especially. He's made a fortune trading himself off as this character. But now he has to live with the character he's created. He's rich, he has everything he needs. But he's cut off from the world. He's trapped in his creation — it imbues his relationship to everything. He knows at some level life is lacking something, but he's too far gone to know exactly what it is. Instead, he walks around that big house of his, waiting for things to feel alright again. That man will be waiting forever."

237

"I know the feeling," Rachel said, pulling Stuart towards her. "Last week was too long: maybe I should join you in Paris."

"Maybe you should," said Stuart. They kissed again, a more tender kiss of calmed nerves. The rain began to fall more heavily. "Shall we get a drink?" Stuart asked, eyeing a nearby pub.

"Definitely," said Rachel. They huddled together and ducked into the inviting light of an old London inn.

35

Odilio was leaving the deli when he received a call from Cooper. "Odilio, you bugger! I just had a flick through that Pickled Aubergine piece." His editor let out a hacking cough. "Could we have a chat?"

"Of course," said Odilio with rising excitement. It would be the only feedback he'd receive for the review. Just a few evenings before, Odilio had deleted Twitter and asked that, from now on, his assistant deal with his emails. Odilio would be contactable only by phone, answering only the numbers he knew. It would save years of his life he'd otherwise lose in turmoil. Safe to say, he craved a quieter existence these days.

"It wasn't very you," said his editor. Odilio could hear the hesitation in his voice. "I was waiting for the punchline. I've nothing against vegan restaurants, of course, I just assumed you did…"

"Right," said Odilio. He didn't feel the fight in him. With Cooper, it was sometimes best to bite your tongue. Odilio disengaged as his editor gave a pep talk of the sort a PE teacher had once delivered to greater effect. Just as Odilio was feeling about his pockets for his house keys, there was a change in his editor's tone: an unnatural use of the preterite tense, something strained in that voice… Was his editor breaking up with him?

239

"I've had the shareholders on my case all week. Everything's going digital. Look, Odilio, why don't you swing by the office tomorrow, and we'll have a proper chat here."

"I'm happy to chat now—"

"It's really not something I like to discuss on the phone."

"I feel *more* comfortable talking about these things on the phone."

His boss sighed. "It's nothing personal, the shareholders want you out. They crack the whip. I'll be straight with you, they want half of us gone by Christmas. A new direction for the magazine, or some bollocks. What they're offering is very generous. You've still got two months on contract, then another eight for remuneration. I'd take it. Go somewhere nice for a bit, lie in the sun. All the rags will be fighting for you when you're back. Sorry to be the bearer of bad news."

Odilio suspected he was still in shock as he filled the fridge with items from the deli and whistled a highland tune as he made his way around the kitchen island to scoop up his wife in a hug. She was watching a video about Japanese whaling on her iPad. She said nothing, smiled and pecked Odilio on the cheek before returning her attention to it. Odilio switched the kettle on for a cup of tea. He watched Helena as the kettle steamed and bubbled until the lever on the side flicked up. He took his tea to the study and switched on his computer, typing 'chess' into the browser. This was how he was spending his free time off of Twitter. Online chess with people around the world. He was even teaching himself tactics on YouTube.

240

Odilio felt a pleasant nothingness as he dragged the white pawn to the e4 square. Contrary to his preconceptions of the game — the notion of chess players planning several moves ahead — Odilio considered it a game of feeling more than thought. There was something intuitive in his control of the pieces. Sometimes, it felt as if there was no barrier between his brain and their position on the board. The board became an expression of his mind. Chess was a staple of his afternoons. The mental investment of playing was like an anaesthetic. Sitting there, staring at the screen with its sixty-four black and white squares, Odilio thought nothing of the call he'd just received. He was not thinking about who he'd have to tell, or how he would tell them; what he imagined they'd think and how this could be dissonant in their reaction. Clicking the pieces on the board, he thought briefly of a story he'd enjoyed as a child. A young man was placed under a spell that would turn him into a toad unless he walked to a new town every night. He was never allowed to revisit the same place — he could never go back to the same house or see the same people. Every day, he continued onwards, never repeating his experiences, unable to apply what he'd learnt from his mistakes, doomed to keep making new ones. Details of the story escaped Odilio's memory, but its summary survived, becoming crisper in its conclusory impact as time passed.

Odilio was thinking about the wandering young man as he sat in his study that afternoon. The future was an open book, the pages of which didn't need filling out with some grand narrative. A series of short sketches could suffice: some important notes in the margins, the odd poem. He would grow vegetables. Nothing too involved — a small plot of land to begin with. There would be more time with his daughter. More time with Helena. More time to read books. No longer wasting time with things he didn't care about.

He glanced up at the gurning head of the boar. Now, he remembered the aftermath of that day, driving it back to the cottage, the creature wrapped in newspaper, bleeding out onto his lap. His father wouldn't tolerate crying. He remembered, now, how he'd fought to keep the tears in. There were two paths you could take in those sorts of moments: you could cry or change your worldview. Or maybe the two paths become one? Moisture was building in Odilio's eyes. It was a sadness that was impossible to pinpoint. An exhuming of memory and feeling. For what he'd done and what he hadn't. For missing people. For himself and everyone else. There are no one-size-fits-all aphorisms. You walk the line. His wet eyes made mosaic tiles of the computer screen. Looking up at the wall again, he decided he would take all those animal heads down when he was finished.

36

"Lift off!" Helena squealed, as the craneman radioed his colleague in the street. The crane whirred as it kicked into gear. The large sculpture — the principal fixture of the late Elias Karlsson's seminal Hearts exhibition — swayed gently as it rose into the air, before exiting seamlessly out the window. "You know, I think I'll miss it," said Helena, as they stared at the empty space the sculpture had occupied. "I'd grown rather fond of it, to be honest."

Shortly after Elias' funeral, Sylvie Dupont had emailed Helena, letting her know how touched she'd been to have met the young artist so close to the end of his life. Days later she flew to London, where they'd shared drinks and discussed his work in detail. Before leaving, Sylvie secured purchase of *Come and Get It* for an undisclosed seven-figure sum. It was posthumously renamed *A Requiem for All the Beautiful Things in the Sky.*

After taxes, the profits of the sale were split 95:5 between The Courtenay Estate and The Elias Trust, where it was made as a special contribution on behalf of Helena as a tax-deductible donation. Sylvie Dupont went on to sell the sculpture to an anonymous art collector in the Persian Gulf. It was destroyed on transit through the Arabian sea and compensated with a 50% mark-up of its value as part of an exclusive insurance deal. What was left of Hearts would go on to exhibit internationally in over forty countries.

Samuel Mills is a writer from London. He is the author of numerous short stories, including the 2017 collection, Nightmares. Poacher's Priest is his first novel.

Printed in Great Britain
by Amazon